EIGHTY ENGLISH FOLK SONGS

Eighty English Folk Songs
from the Southern Appalachians

COLLECTED BY CECIL SHARP AND MAUD KARPELES

EDITED BY MAUD KARPELES

CHORD SYMBOLS BY PAT SHAW

SPECIMEN PIANO ACCOMPANIMENTS BY BENJAMIN BRITTEN

FABER MUSIC
in association with
FABER AND FABER
London and Boston

First published in 1968
by Faber and Faber Limited
in association with Faber Music Limited
3 Queen Square London WC1
Printed in Great Britain by
Martin's of Berwick

ISBN 0 571 10048 1

CONTENTS

INTRODUCTION

THE EIGHTY songs in this volume have been selected from a collection of about five hundred, or over 1,600 including variants, which Cecil Sharp and I made in the Southern Appalachian Mountains during the years 1916 to 1918.*

The Appalachian mountain system runs parallel with the eastern seaboard of the North American continent and lies about 250 miles inland. Our hunting ground lay in the States of North Carolina, Tennessee, Virginia and Kentucky. The inhabitants of these mountains are of British descent—English, Scots and Scots–Irish—their ancestors having left their native shores about two hundred years or so ago. They transported little from the Old Country in the way of material goods, but they brought with them the priceless possession of their traditional songs which they carried not in books but in their hearts and minds; and these songs have been treasured and have been handed down by word of mouth through the successive generations.

The country we explored included the ranges of the Great Smokies, Black Mountains, Blue Ridge and Cumberland Mountains. The mountains, which are covered with virgin forest, rise up steeply from the mountain valleys; and until recently they have acted as a barrier between the mountain communities and the outside world. At the time that Cecil Sharp and I were there it was a very difficult country to get about in. There were hardly any proper roads, but just rough tracks over the mountains or alongside the rivers; and often the only roadway for some miles would be the actual bed of the river.

The people lived in primitive log-cabins dotted along the banks of the rivers, or creeks as they were called. They were very nearly self-supporting, building their own log-cabins, spinning and weaving the wool for their clothes and growing their own food. Their living was not luxurious, but they had leisure and that they prized more than material comfort and possessions.

There were only a few schools and most of the people could neither read nor write; but although they had had but little formal education they possessed a fine inherited culture. This was shown in the pattern of their social behaviour, their dignified bearing, their racy and intelligent conversation and, above all, in their songs. During the forty-six weeks we spent in the mountains we never heard a bad tune, except for the occasional hymn that had strayed from one of the missionary settlements. We felt we were living in a really musical atmosphere. Yet there was no such thing as a concert in the mountains, nor even community singing or a folk-song club.

---

* More than half the songs, i.e. 274 separate songs and 968 tunes including variants, are published in *English Folk Songs from the Southern Appalachians*, collected by Cecil J. Sharp, edited by Maud Karpeles (Oxford University Press, London, 1932, 1960). This publication also includes an account of the singers and their songs and gives references to other versions of the songs.

Singing was just part of everyday life. People sang for their own enjoyment or for that of their immediate circle of friends and relations. It would often happen that we would hear a voice in the distance and then, following it up, we would find, perhaps, a man singing as he hoed his corn-patch, or a girl milking a cow, or a woman nursing her baby. Owing to their isolation, the mountain people had been preserved from commercialized music and the songs they had inherited from their forefathers had been evolved according to the taste of the singers themselves without any extraneous influence.

Cecil Sharp was first introduced to the songs through Mrs John C. Campbell who had herself noted between seventy and eighty songs some years previously. It was at her suggestion that he decided to prospect the mountain region. The result far exceeded his wildest imagination. Fifty years ago, folk music in England had gone underground, so to speak, and it was mainly from the memories of the old people that Cecil Sharp had to unearth the songs. In the Appalachian Mountains, there awaited him a folk-song collector's paradise; for there nearly every one sang, old and young alike, and when they sang it was nearly always a folk song of English origin.

We travelled through the mountains, generally on foot, staying in the homes of the people or at a missionary settlement and calling, usually without introduction, at any dwelling that lay on our way. Strangers such as ourselves were rare, but good manners never allowed those we met to show the slightest sign of surprise and we were received everywhere with the greatest friendliness and hospitality. Our collecting was done before the days of the tape recorder. Cecil Sharp took down the tunes in ordinary staff notation and I noted the words: a combined operation that afforded great delight to our singers.

And what of the songs? There is no need to say much about them here, for they speak for themselves. And the better we get to know them, the more they have to say to us. They never pall and one is constantly discovering fresh beauties in them.

The songs were, with one exception, sung without instrumental accompaniment. This is in accordance with the older traditional method of singing, both in England and in America. The present custom of singing to the accompaniment of guitar or banjo, which has been adopted by some traditional singers, is fairly recent and is probably due to the influence of popular and pseudo-folk music heard on the radio. This tonic-dominant form of accompaniment is in most cases quite unsuited to the structure of the melody and has the effect of ironing out its distinctive qualities.

The songs were conceived as melodic entities and are not dependent on harmonic support; but this is not to imply that a harmonic or contrapuntal arrangement is necessarily incompatible with their nature. In the hands of a skilled and sympathetic musician the songs may be transmuted into another medium which can be completely satisfying. The specimen pianoforte accompaniments by Benjamin Britten which are contained in this book offer fruitful suggestions for ways in which the songs can be treated, as do the chord symbols supplied for some of the songs by

Pat Shaw. These accompaniments will meet the need of singers who feel that they require the support of an accompanying instrument, and I am most grateful to Mr Britten and to Mr Shaw for their generous and distinguished collaboration. We would, however, suggest that before having recourse to an accompaniment singers should first familiarize themselves with the song so as to avoid starting off with a preconceived harmonic conception of it.

The recent building of roads and the introduction of electricity have brought great changes in the lives of the mountain people and they now enjoy material advantages which were absent fifty years ago. But the changes are not all to the good. Markets are now accessible and people are so busy earning a living that they have not the leisure in which to enjoy living, as they had in the past. Then again, community life has been disturbed and traditional values have been upset. People feel that they have got to keep up with the times, and the latest 'hits' which are heard on the radio are taking the place of the beautiful songs they grew up with. Yet they will admit that their own songs are better and it takes but little encouragement for them to start searching their memories for them. I have been back to the mountains twice since I was there with Cecil Sharp and have visited some of our former singers and their children. When I have shown them their own or their parents' songs printed in Cecil Sharp's book, they have been overjoyed and the songs have thereupon taken on a new lease of life.

Owing to changed social conditions the songs are no longer able to survive solely by means of oral transmission; but that does not mean that they are of any less value or are out-dated. The best folk songs—and those in this book can surely be accounted such—are ageless, as is all great art, and they have the power to transcend the particular circumstances which obtained when they were created. It is our hope that these songs will become the property of all English-speaking people and they they will not be reserved for special occasions, but will be bound up with everyday life as they once were in the Appalachian Mountains.

MAUD KARPELES
London, 1968

SPECIMEN PIANO ACCOMPANIMENTS
by BENJAMIN BRITTEN

LOVE HENRY (*Young Hunting*)

WHAT'S LITTLE BABIES MADE OF?

What's old wo-men made of, made of? What's old wo-men made of? _____ Reels and jeels and old spin-ning wheels And that's what old wo — men are made of.

THE MAID FREED FROM THE GALLOWS

O— hang man, O hang man, O hold up your rope, And

hold it— for— a—— while. I think I— see my

fa — ther— dear A — com-ing a ma-ny long mile.

THE FROG AND THE MOUSE

The frog went a-court-ing and he did ride, H'm!
h'm! The frog went a-court-ing and he did ride With his
sword and his pis-tol by his side. H'm! ____

Repeat to first
or second bar-
ad libitum.

A NOTE FOR GUITARISTS

When they were collected, none of these songs were accompanied and this is still the ideal way of performing them. However, there are many ways of harmonizing them which do not interfere with their essential characteristics. The chord symbols given here are simply suggestions and it is hoped that they may provide a basis on which guitarists or other instrumentalists can build their own accompaniments. One word of warning. It is possible, even easy, to produce harmonizations that are so fascinating in their own right that the listener is more conscious of the accompaniment than of the melody and words. Beware of becoming too elaborate: it is the song itself that matters.

Remember this too when deciding on the rhythmic style for an accompaniment. It is the current fashion to produce very 'busy' accompaniments, but simple rhythms are generally more effective. A quiet rippling figure, provided it is not obtrusive, can be a good background to show up the song, but do not forget also the value of plain chords. While some songs in this collection naturally benefit from strong rhythmic support, many are in a very free style and forcing them into a definite rhythm kills their very nature. Always make your accompaniment fit the song: never force a song into a pre-conceived accompaniment.

The singer playing his own accompaniments should keep well within the limitations of his technique; he should be free to concentrate on the song and not have to think too much about what his fingers are doing. In the early stages of learning the guitar, players are often content just to strum chords in any position. As soon as possible they should try to learn chords in all their inversions; this will enable them to produce a far more interesting bass line and a more sensitive, less 'corny' type of accompaniment. To this end, in some places the actual bass note has been suggested by a small letter placed under the capital letter chord symbol. For example, $\frac{G}{b}$ represents the first inversion of the chord G major, i.e. with the note B at the bottom of the chord. Occasionally alternative or optional harmonies are given in brackets.

On the whole, keys suitable for the guitar have been chosen, but if it is found that a particular song is too low, it is easy to transpose it up with a capo: putting it down, on the other hand, is sometimes very awkward. (If the songs are being sung unaccompanied, transposition to a key to suit the individual voice is an easy matter once the song has been learnt.) Nevertheless, it has not been found possible to avoid altogether chords requiring a barré. Many guitarists in the learning stage fight shy of this. All we would say it that with a little practice and perseverance the technical difficulties will soon be overcome and as it opens the door to such a much wider range of harmonic possibilities it is well worth the effort.

The following diagrams show easy fingerings for some of the less familiar chords given in the songs. The numbers refer to the left-hand fingers: x over a string indicates that it should not be played.

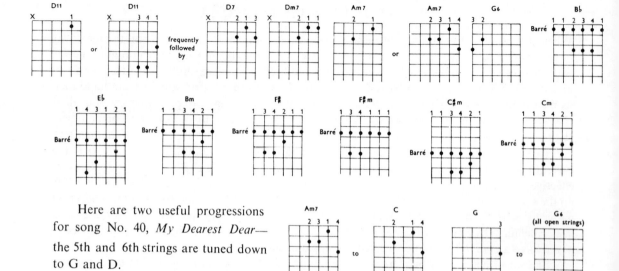

Here are two useful progressions for song No. 40, *My Dearest Dear*— the 5th and 6th strings are tuned down to G and D.

Two songs in contrasting rhythmical styles will illustrate the way in which the bass notes, indicated by small letters, can be used in the accompaniments. The first is No. 34, *William and Polly*.

It would be possible, of course, to stick to a ♩ ♪♩ ♪ rhythm throughout, but it makes for variety and is not too fussy to break it sometimes, as has been done here.

The second song is No. 31, *Locks and Bolts*. These two ideas for the accompaniment can be used either separately or in combination.

Come men and maids and lis-ten a while; I'll tell you a -

- bout my dar - ling. She's the lit - tle one I __ love_ so

well; She's al - most the com — plete one.

17

A repeated pattern of notes or ostinato makes an effective accompaniment for some songs. Here is a suggestion for No. 69, *Nottamun Town*. (Note that the ostinato here does not correspond to the chord symbols, but is an alternative form of accompaniment.) The tone colour can be varied by plucking the strings in different places—near the finger-board, over the sound-hole or close to the bridge.

A drone accompaniment suits other songs, No. 11, *The Two Brothers*, for example. Plain spread chords are effective but can become slightly monotonous, particularly in a ballad like this with many verses; so for variety a contrasting arpeggio style of accompaniment can be introduced where the bass notes differ from bar to bar. (Note that the 6th string is tuned down to D.)

Here are some other possible figurations for the same song. In the latter two, Th means a thumb stroke across all six strings and F a stroke with the forefinger in the direction of the arrow. (In these examples, too, the 6th string is tuned down to D.)

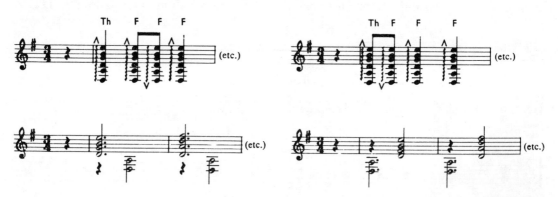

All these different figurations can be combined with each other, and there are many other possibilities which can be learnt from the various Folk Guitar tutors and records. No hard-and-fast rules can be given for working out accompaniments. Each song must be treated on its own, and different ideas, both rhythmic and harmonic, tried out until a satisfying combination is achieved. Sometimes this comes easily and naturally, sometimes only after much experimenting and hard work; but the result should always be a fitting background to a song and not an instrumental solo with vocal accompaniment.

PAT SHAW
London, 1968

20

1 THE LOVERS' TASKS
(*The Elfin Knight*)

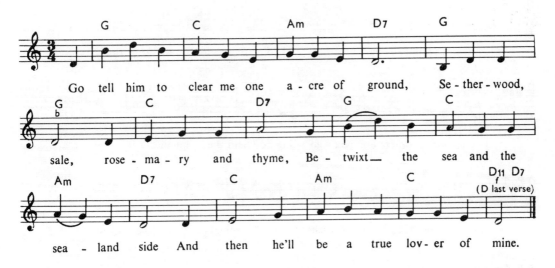

Go tell him to clear me one a-cre of ground, Se-ther-wood,
sale, rose-ma-ry and thyme, Be-twixt the sea and the
sea - land side And then he'll be a true lov-er of mine.

Go tell him to plough it with a plough of old
    leather,
Setherwood, sale, rosemary and thyme,
And hoe it all over with a pea-fowl's feather,
    And then he'll be a true lover of mine.

Go tell him to plant it with one grain of corn,
    Setherwood, sale, rosemary and thyme,
And reap it all down with an old ram's horn,
    And then he'll be a true lover of mine.

Go tell her to make me a cambric shirt,
    Setherwood, sale, rosemary and thyme,
Without any needle or needle's work,
    And then she'll be a true lover of mine.

Go tell her to wash it in yonders well,
    Setherwood, sale, rosemary and thyme,
Where never was water nor rain never fell,
    And then she'll be a true lover of mine.

Go tell her to hang it on yonders thorn,
    Setherwood, sale, rosemary and thyme,
Which never bore leaf since Adam was born,
    And then she'll be a true lover of mine.

2 THE FALSE KNIGHT UPON THE ROAD

The knight met a child in the road.

O where are you go-ing to? Said the knight in the road.

I'm a-go-ing to my school, Said the child as he stood. He

stood and he stood, And it's well be-cause he stood. I'm a-go-ing

to my school, Said the child as he stood.

O what are you going there for?
  Said the knight in the road.
For to learn the Word of God,
  Said the child as he stood.
He stood and he stood,
  And it's well because he stood.
For to learn the Word of God,
  Said the child as he stood.

O what have you got there?
  Said the knight in the road.
I have got my bread and cheese,
  Said the child as he stood.
He stood and he stood, *etc.*

O won't you give me some?
No, ne'er a bite nor crumb.

O I wish you were on the sands.
Yes, and a good staff in my hands.

O I wish you were in the sea.
Yes, and a good boat under me.

O I think I hear a bell.
Yes, and it's ringing you to hell.

3 THE SEVEN SLEEPERS
(*Earl Brand*)

Wake you up, wake you up, you_ sev'n sleep - - ers, And_ do take warn-ing by me. O do take care of your old-est daugh-ter dear, For the young-est is go-ing with me.

Lady Marg'ret she mounted her milk-white steed,
Lord William his dapple grey.
He drew his buckler down by his side,
And so he went riding away.

He rode, he rode that livelong day
Along with his lady so dear
Until he saw her seven brothers bold
And her father a-walking so near.

Light off, light off, Lady Marg'ret, he said,
And hold my reins in your hand
Till I go fight your seven brothers bold
And your father by them stand.

She held, she held, O she better, better held
And she never shed one tear
Until she saw her seven brothers fall
And her father she loved so dear.

She pulléd out her silk handkerchief,
Which was both soft and fine,
And she wipéd off her father's bloody wounds
Till they ran more clearer than wine.

Lady Marg'ret she mounted her milk-white steed,
Lord William his dapple grey.
He drew his buckler down by his side,
And so he went bleeding away.

They rode, they rode, O they better, better rode,
They rode by the light of the moon
Until they came to his own mother's door,
Crying: Rise and let us come in.

O mother, O mother, go make my bed,
And fix it wide and smooth;
And lay my true love down by my side
So that we may rest for a while.

Lord William he died about midnight,
Lady Marg'ret a while before day.
And I hope every couple that may ever come
  together
May see more pleasure than they.

4 THE OUTLANDISH KNIGHT

(*Lady Isabel and the Elf Knight*)

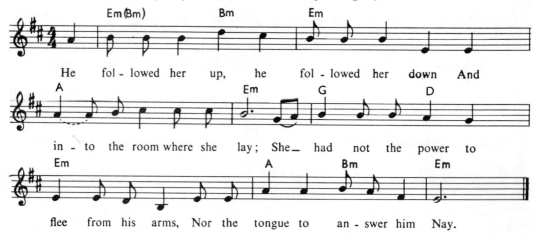

He fol-lowed her up, he fol-lowed her down And
in-to the room where she lay; She had not the power to
flee from his arms, Nor the tongue to an-swer him Nay.

Come rise you up, my pretty Polly,
And go along with me;
I'll take you to the North Scotland
And married we will be.

Go.bring me a bag of your father's gold,
Likewise your mother's fee,
And the two best horses out of the stall,
Where there stand thirty and three.

She lit upon her nimble going brown;
He mounted the dapple grey;
And when they reached the North Scotland
'Twas just three hours till day.

Light you down, light you down, my pretty Polly,
Light you down, I say unto thee.
It's six king's daughters here have I drowned
And you the seventh shall be.

Pull off, pull off those fine gay clothes
And hang them on yonder tree,
For they are too fine and they cost too much
For to rot in the salt lake sea.

Go get those sickles for to cut those nettles
That grow so close to the brim,
For they may tangle in my long yellow hair
And tear my snowy white skin.

He got those sickles for to cut those nettles
That grow so close to the brim.
She picked him up and so skilfully
She plunged false William in.

Lie there, lie there, you false William,
Lie there in the room of me;
For six king's daughters you have drowned
And you the seventh shall be.

She rode upon the nimble going brown
And led the dapple grey;
She rode till she came to her father's gate,
'Twas just three hours till day.

Hush up, hush up, you pretty parrot bird,
Don't tell no tales on me.
Your cage shall be made of the yellow beaten gold
And the doors of ivory.

Up speaks, up speaks that good old man
From the chamber where he lay;
What's the matter with my pretty parrot bird,
She's talking so long before day?

Here sit three cats at my cage door,
My life they will betray;
And I'm just calling for pretty Polly
To drive those cats away.

5 THE TWO CROWS
(*The Three Ravens*)

The old he-crow said to his mate,
  Lardy hip tie hoddy ho ho,
The old he-crow said to his mate:
What shall we have today to eat?
  Lardy hardy hip tie hoddy ho ho.

There lies a horse in yonders lane
Whose body has not long been slain.

We'll press our feet on his breast-bone,
And pick his eyes out one by one.

6 THE TWO SISTERS

There lived a lord in the North Coun-tree, Bow down, There

lived a lord in the North Countree, Bow— down to me, There

lived a lord in the North Coun-tree And he had daugh-ters one, two, three.

I'll be true—to my love If my love be true to me.

A young man came a-courting there,
  Bow down,
A young man came a-courting there,
  Bown down to me,
A young man came a-courting there,
And he made choice of the youngest there
  I'll be true to my love
  If my love be true to me.

He gave the youngest a gay gold ring;
He never bought the oldest a single thing.

O sister, O sister, let us walk out
To see the ships a-sailing about.

As they walked down to the salty brim,
The oldest pushed the youngest in.

O sister, O sister, lend me your hand
And I will give you my house and land.

I'll neither lend you my hand nor glove,
But I will have your own true love.

O down she sank and away she swam
And into the miller's fish-pond she ran.

The miller came out with his fish-hook
And he fished the fair maid out of the brook.

He robbed her of her gay gold ring
And into the brook he pushed her again.

The miller was hung at his mill-gate;
The oldest sister was burned at the stake.

7 JOHN RANDOLPH
(*Lord Randal*)

Where have you been a – rov-ing, John Ran-dolph, my son?

Where have you been a – rov-ing? Pray tell me, lit - tle one. I've

been out a —— court-ing. Go —— make my bed soon.

Mo-ther, I'm sick at the heart and I want to lie down.

What did you have for your supper, John
Randolph, my son?
What did you have for your supper? Pray tell me,
little one.
Had eel soup and vinegar. Go make my bed soon.
Mother, I'm sick to the heart and I want to lie
down.

What colour was it, *etc.*
It was brown and brown-speckled, *etc.*

What'll you will to your father?
My mules and my wagons.

What'll you will to your mother?
My coach and six horses.

What'll you will to your brother?
My hounds and my musket.

What'll you will to your sister?
My rings off my fingers.

What'll you will to your sweetheart?
A cup of strong poison.

Note
The rhythm of this song is very free. Where the first two notes of the bar are indicated as ♪♩. they

should each be given rather more than their face value, i.e. approximately ♩ ♩

8 EDWARD

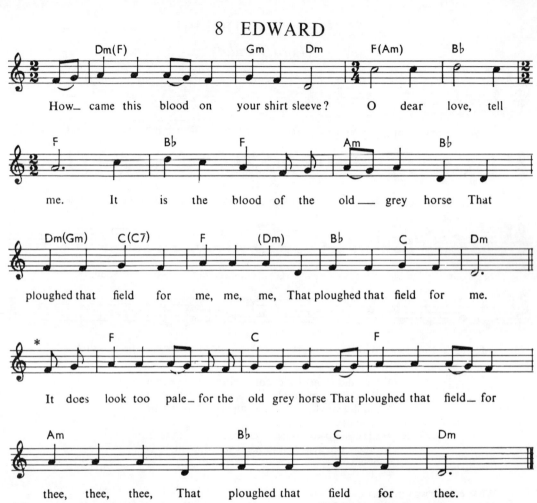

How— came this blood on your shirt sleeve? O dear love, tell

me. It is the blood of the old — grey horse That

ploughed that field for me, me, me, That ploughed that field for me.

It does look too pale— for the old grey horse That ploughed that field— for

thee, thee, thee, That ploughed that field for thee.

How came this blood on your shirt sleeve?
  O dear love, tell me..
It is the blood of the old grey hound
That traced that fox for me, me, me,
That traced that for for me.
It does look too pale for the old greyhound
That traced that fox for thee, thee, thee;
That traced that fox for thee.

How came this blood on your shirt sleeve?
  O dear love, tell me.
It is the blood of my brother-in-law
That went away with me, me, me,
That went away with me.

* The following six bars are sung in verses 1 and 2 only.

And it's what did you fall out about?
  O dear love, tell me.
About a little bit of bush
That soon would have made a tree, tree, tree,
That soon would have made a tree.

And it's what will you do now, my love?
  O dear love, tell me.
I'll set my foot in yonders ship
And I'll sail across the sea, sea, sea,
And I'll sail across the sea.

And it's when will you come back, my love?
  O dear love, tell me.
When the sun sets into yonder sycamore tree,
And that shall never be, be, be,
And that shall never be.

9 THE CRUEL MOTHER

There was a la-dy near the town, All a-lone, a-lone-y,____ She

walked all night and all a-round. All down by the green-wood side-y.____

She leaned herself against a thorn,
  All alone, aloney,
Two sweet little babes to her were born.
  All down by the greenwood sidey.

She got a rope both long and neat
And tied them down both hands and feet.

She got a knife both keen and sharp
And pierced it through each tender heart.

As she went out one moonlit night
She saw two babes all dressed in white.

O babes, O babes, if you were mine,
I'd dress you up in silk so fine.

O mother, O mother, when we were thine,
You neither dressed us coarse nor fine.

In seven years you'll hear a bell,
In seven years you'll land in hell.

10 LORD BATEMAN
(*Young Beichan*)

Lord Bate-man was a — no - ble lord__ And he was__

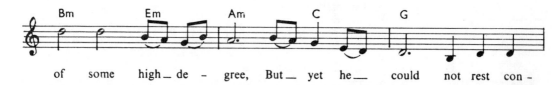

of some high __ de - gree, But __ yet he __ could not rest con -

- tent-ed, Some fo - reign __ coun - tries __ he __ would see.

He sailéd East and he sailéd West
Until he came to proud Turkey,
Where he was caught and put in prison
Until his life grew quite weary.

The Turk he had one only daughter,
The fairest creature eyes did see,
She stole the keys of her father's prison
And said: Lord Bateman I will free.

Have you got houses, have you got land
And are you of some high degree?
And what will you give to the fair young lady
That out of prison will set you free?

Yes, I've got houses and I've got land
And half Northumb'land belongs to me
And I'll give it all to the fair young lady
That out of prison will set me free.

She took him to her father's table
And gave to him the best of wine,
And every health she drank unto him:
I wish, Lord Bateman, you were mine.

She led him to her father's harbour
And gave to him a ship of fame.
Farewell, farewell, to you, Lord Bateman,
Farewell, farewell, till we meet again.

It's seven long years I'll make this bargain,
It's seven long years I'll give my hand;
If you will wed no other woman
Then I will wed no other man.

When seven long years had come and gone
And fourteen days well known to thee,
She dressed herself in her fine gay clothing
And says: Lord Bateman I'll go see.

And when she came to Lord Bateman's castle
She tingled loudly at the bell.
Who's there, who's there? cried the proud young
   porter,
Who's there, who's there? Unto me tell.

She said: Is this Lord Bateman's castle
And is his lordship here within?
O yes, this is Lord Bateman's castle.
He's just now taken a young bride in.

Go tell him to send me a slice of cake,
A bottle of the best of wine,
And not to forget the fair young lady
That did release him from close confine.

Away, away went the proud young porter,
Until Lord Bateman he did see.
What news, what news, my proud young porter,
What news, what news have you brought to me?

There stands at your gate the fairest lady
That ever my two eyes did see.
She has a ring on every finger
And on one of them she has got three.

She says to bring her a slice of cake,
A bottle of the best of wine,
And not to forget the fair young lady
That did release you from close confine.

Lord Bateman then in a passion flew,
His sword he broke in pieces three.
O I'll forsake my house and living
If Sophie has a-crossed the sea.

It's up then spoke the young bride's mother
Who was never heard to speak so free:
O don't forsake my only daughter
Though Sophie has a-crossed the sea.

I own I've made a bride of your daughter,
I'm sure she's none the worse by me;
She came here on a horse and saddle,
I'll send her home in a coach and three.

Lord Bateman prepared another wedding;
And both their hearts are full of glee.
I'll range no more to foreign countries
Now Sophie has a-crossed the sea.

11 THE TWO BROTHERS

There were two_ bro-thers a - go-ing to school, A-
-go-ing to the ve-ry same school. The old-est says_ to the
young-est one: Let's take a_ wres-tle and fall.

The very first fall the old one gave,
He threw him to the ground;
And from his pocket he drew a knife
And gave him a deathly wound.

Pull off, pull off, your woollen shirt
And tear it from gore to gore
And wrap it around this deathly wound
That it may bleed no more.

It's he pulled off his woollen shirt
And tore it from gore to gore
And wrapped it around this deathly wound
And it did bleed no more.

Pick me up, pick me up all in your arms
And carry me to yonders church ground
And dig my grave both wide and deep
And gently lay me down.

He picked him up all in his arms
And carried him to yonders church ground
And dug his grave both wide and deep
And gently laid him down.

What must I tell my father dear
This evening as I go home?
Just tell him I'm a-learning young hounds to run
Down in some lonesome grove.

What must I tell my mother dear
This evening as I go home?
Just tell her I'm in the old school-house
With a long, long lesson to learn.

What must I tell your own true love
This evening as I go home?
Just tell her I'm in my silent grave
And never no more to return.

They buried his Bible at his head,
His prayer-book at his feet,
His bow and arrow by his side,
And now he lies asleep.

Note
Guitarists can tune the 6th string down to D and, using the 5th and 6th strings as a drone throughout,
finger the chords only on the top three or four strings.
See p. 19 for specimen accompaniment.

12 THE CHERRY TREE CAROL

When Jo - seph was a young man, A — young man was he, He —
court - ed Vir - gin Ma - ry, The — Queen of Ga - li - lee, He —
court - ed Vir - gin Ma - ry, The — Queen of Ga - li - lee.

As Joseph and Mary
Were walking one day,
There were apples and cherries, } (bis)
A-plenty to behold.

Then Mary spoke to Joseph
So meek and so mild:
Joseph, gather me some cherries
For I am with child.

Then Joseph flew in angry,
In angry he flew.
Let the father of the baby
Gather cherries for you.

Lord Jesus spoke these few words
All from his mother's womb:
Bow low down, you cherry tree,
Let my mother have some.

The cherry tree bowed low down,
Low down to the ground,
And Mary gathered cherries
While Joseph stood around.

Then Joseph took Mary
All on his right knee,
Crying: Lord have mercy on me
For what I have done.

Then Joseph took Mary
All on his left knee.
Pray tell me, little baby,
When your birthday will be?

On the fifth day of January
My birthday will be,
When the stars and the elements
Do tremble with fear.

13 LOVE HENRY
(*Young Hunting*)

Light you down, light you down, love Hen-ry, she said, And__ stay all__ night with

me, For I have a bed and a fire - side too And a

can - dle a - burn-ing bright, And a can - dle a - burn- ing bright.__

I won't get down, nor I can't get down
And stay all night with thee,
For that little girl in the old Declarn
Would think so hard of me. (*bis*)

But he slided down from his saddle skirts
For to kiss her snowy white cheek.
She had a sharp knife in her hand
And she plunged it in him deep.

I will get down and I can get down
And stay all night with thee,
For there's no little girl in the old Declarn
That I love any better than thee.

Must I ride to the East, must I ride to the West,
Or anywhere under the sun,
To get some good and clever doctor
For to cure this wounded man?

Neither ride to the East, neither ride to the West,
Nor nowhere under the sun,
For there's no man but God's own hand
Can cure this wounded man.

She took him by the long yellow locks
And also round the feet;
She plunged him in that doleful well
Some sixty fathoms deep.

And as she turned around to go home
She heard some pretty bird sing:
Go home, go home, you cruel girl,
Lament and mourn for him.

Fly down, fly down, pretty parrot, she said,
Fly down and go home with me.
Your cage shall be decked with beads of gold
And hung in the willow tree.

For specimen piano accompaniment see page 11

I won't fly down, nor I can't fly down,
And I won't go home with thee,
For you have murdered your own true love
And you might murder me.

I wish I had my little bow-ben
And had it with a string;
I'd surely shoot that cruel bird
That sits on the briers and sings.

I wish you had your little bow-ben
And had it with a string;
I'd surely fly from vine to vine;
You could always hear me sing.

14 THE MAID FREED FROM THE GALLOWS

O— hang-man, O hang – man, O hold up your rope, And hold it — for — a — while. I think I— see my fa – ther— dear A – com – ing a ma-ny long mile.

O father, O father, O have you any gold,
Or silver to pay my fee?
They say I've stolen a silver cup
And hangéd I must be.

No daughter, no daughter, I've got no gold for
    thee,
Nor silver to pay your fee;
But I've come here to see you hang
On yon high gallows tree.

*In subsequent verses, 'mother', 'brother', 'sister'
and finally 'true love' are substituted for 'father'.
The last verse runs thus:*

Yes, true love, yes, true love, I have got gold for
    thee
And silver to pay your fee,
And I've come here to win your neck
From yon high gallows tree.

For specimen piano accompaniment see page 13

15 LORD THOMAS AND FAIR ELLINOR

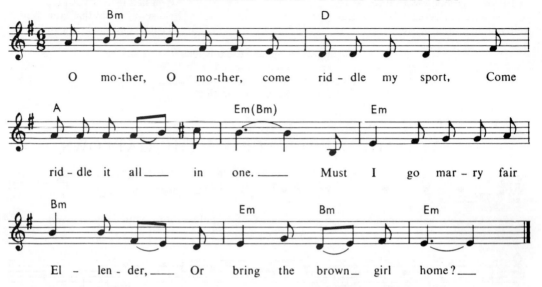

O mo-ther, O mo-ther, come rid-dle my sport, Come
rid-dle it all ___ in one. ___ Must I go mar-ry fair
El – len-der, ___ Or bring the brown ___ girl home? ___

The brown girl she has house and land,
Fair Ellender she has none;
And my advice would be for you
To bring the brown girl home.

He dressed himself in scarlet red
And wore a robe of green;
And every town that he passed through
They took him to be some king.

He rode up to fair Ellender's gate,
He jingled at the ring;
And none so ready as fair Ellender
To rise and let him in.

What news, what news, Lord Thomas? she cried.
What news do you bring to me?
I come to bid you to my wedding
And that's sad news to thee.

O mother, O mother, come riddle my sport,
Come riddle it all in one.
Must I go to Lord Thomas's wedding,
Or stay at home and mourn?

There may be many of your friends,
But many more of your foes,
And my advice would be for you
To tarry this day at home.

There may be hundreds of my friends
And thousands of my foes;
Betide my life, betide my death,
To Lord Thomas's wedding I'll go.

She dressed herself in scarlet so fine
And wore a belt of green,
And every town that she rode through
They took her to be some queen.

She rode up to Lord Thomas's gate,
She jingled at the ring;
And none so ready as Lord Thomas himself
To rise and let her in.

He took her by the lily-white hand
And led her across the hall
And sat her down in a golden chair
Among the ladies all.

Is this your bride, Lord Thomas? she cried.
I see she is quite brown;
And you could have married as fair a lady
As ever the sun shone on.

The brown girl had a little penknife
Which was both keen and sharp;
Betwixt the long ribs and the short
She pierced fair Ellender's heart.

O what is the matter? Lord Thomas he cried.
What makes you look so wan?
You used to wear as good a colour
As ever the sun shone on.

O are you blind, Lord Thomas? she cried.
Or can you not very well see?
O can't you see my own heart's blood
Come trinkling down my knee?

He took the brown girl by the hand
And led her across the hall;
And drew his sword and cut off her head
And kicked it against the wall.

He placed the handle against the wall,
The point against his breast.
Here ends the life of three true lovers.
Lord take their souls to rest.

O mother, O mother, go dig my grave,
Go dig it wide and deep;
And place fair Ellender in my arms
And the brown girl at my feet.

16 FAIR MARGARET AND SWEET WILLIAM

Sweet Wil-liam a-rose one May morning And dressed him-self — in blue. Come

tell to me — all a - bout that — love Be - tween La- dy Mar-g'ret and you.

O I know nothing of Lady Marg'ret's love
And she knows nothing of me,
But in the morning at half-past eight
Lady Marg'ret my bride shall see.

Lady Marg'ret was sitting in her bower room
A-combing back her hair;
When who should she spy but Sweet William and
    his bride
As to church they did draw nigh.

Then down she threw her ivory comb,
In silk bound up her hair;
And out of the room this fair lady ran.
She was never any more seen there.

The day passed away and the night coming on
And the most of the men asleep,
Sweet William espied Lady Marg'ret's ghost
A-standing at his bed-feet.

The night passed away and the day coming on
And the most of the men awake,
Sweet William said: I am troubled in my head
By the dream I dreamed last night.

He rode up to Lady Marg'ret's door
And jingled at the ring;
And none so ready as her seventh born brother
To arise and let him in.

O is she in her kitchen room,
Or is she in her hall,
Or is she in her bower room
Among her merry maids all?

She's neither in her kitchen room,
Nor neither in her hall,
But she is in her cold, cold coffin
With her pale face towards the wall.

Pull down, pull down those winding-sheets
A-made of satin so fine.
Ten thousand times you have kissed my lips,
And now, love, I'll kiss thine.

Three times he kissed her snowy white breast,
Three times he kissed her chin;
And when he kissed her cold clay lips
His heart it broke within.

Lady Marg'ret was buried in the old churchyard,
Sweet William was buried close by;
And out of her there sprung a red rose
And out of him a brier.

They grew so tall and they grew so high,
They scarce could grow any higher;
And there they tied in a true lover's knot,
The red rose and the brier.

17 THE THREE LITTLE BABES
(*The Wife of Usher's Well*)

She— had-n't been— mar - ried but a ve - ry short time Till—
chil-dren— she had— three. She— sent them a - way to the north coun -
- tree To— learn _____ their— gram - ma - ree.

They hadn't been there but a very short time,
Scarcely six weeks and three days,
Till sickness came into that old town
And swept her babes away.

She dreamed a dream when the nights were long,
When the nights were long and cold;
She dreamed she saw her three little babes
Come walking down to their home.

She spread them a table on a milk-white cloth
And on it she put cake and wine.
Come and eat, come and eat, my three little babes,
Come and eat and drink of mine.

No mother, no mother, we don't want your cakes,
Nor neither drink your wine,
For yonder stands our Saviour dear
To take us in his arms.

She fixed them a bed in the backside room
And on it she put three sheets,
And one of them was a golden sheet,
Under it that the youngest might sleep.

Take it off, take it off, dear mother, they said,
For we haven't got long to stay,
For yonder stands our Saviour dear,
Where we must surely be.

Dear mother, it's the fruits of your poor proud
heart
That caused us to lie in the clay.
Cold clods at our head, green grass at our feet,
We are wrapped in our winding-sheet.

18 MATTHY GROVES

(*Little Musgrave and Lady Barnard*)

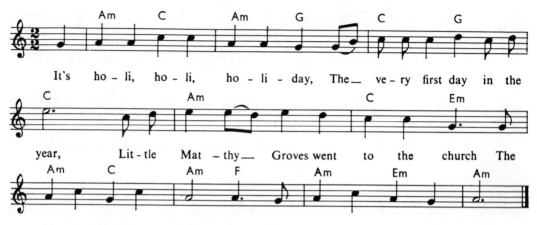

It's ho-li, ho-li, ho-li-day, The—ve-ry first day in the year, Lit-tle Mat—thy— Groves went to the church The Ho-ly Word to hear, hear, The Ho-ly Word to hear.

The first came in wore lily-white,
The next wore pink and blue,
The next came in was Lord Banner's wife,
The flower of the view, view
The flower of the view.

Little Matthy Groves a-being there
All dressed in oil of green,
He looked at her, she looked at him,
The like was never seen.

Come home with me, little Matthy Groves,
Come home with me to-night,
Come home with me, little Matthy Groves,
And sleep with me till light.

O no, O no, I dare not go,
I dare not for my life;
For I know by the rings you wear on your fingers
You are Lord Banner's wife.

And if I am Lord Banner's wife,
Lord Banner's not at home;
He has gone down to the high toll-gate
To call his hirelings home.

The little foot-page was a-standing by
A-hearing what they said.
He swore Lord Banner should have the news
Before the sun should set.

And in his hurry to carry the news
He buckled his shoes as he ran;
And when he came to the river-side
He bent his breast and he swam.

He ran till he came to Lord Banner's hall,
He jingled so loud at the ring.
And none so ready as Lord Banner himself
For to rise and let him in.

What news, what news, my little foot-page,
What news do you bring unto me?
Is any of my castles fallen down,
Or any of my men false been?

There's none of your castles fallen down,
Nor none of your men false been,
But Matthy Groves is sleeping this night
In the arms of your gay lady.

40

If this be a lie your telling to me,
As O I take it to be,
I'll build me a gallows in fair Scotland
And hangéd you shall be.

If this be a lie I'm telling to you,
As O you take it to be,
You need not build no gallows at all;
Just hang me on a tree.

He calléd all his merry men,
By one, by two, by three,
Saying: Let us now go to fair Scotland
This couple for to see.

Then one of Lord Banner's foremost men
Who wished Matthy Groves no ill,
He drew his horn and he blew it loud,
He blew it loud and shrill.

What's this I hear? says little Matthy Groves.
It blew so loud and clear.
I think it is Lord Banner's horn.
O him how do I fear.

Lie down, lie down, little Matthy Groves,
And keep me from the cold;
For it's only my father's shepherd boy
A-calling the sheep to the fold.

They lay and slept, they slumbered and slept,
So sweetly they did sleep;
But when they woke who did they spy
But Lord Banner at their feet.

O how do you like my own bedside,
Or how do you like my sheet?
Or how do you like my gay young wife
Lies in your arms asleep?

Very well I like your own bedside,
Much better do I like your sheet,
But the best of all is your gay young wife
Lies in my arms asleep.

Rise up, rise up, little Matthy Groves,
Rise up, draw on your clothes.
It shall never be said in the fair Scotland
I've slain a naked man.

O no, O no, I dare not rise,
I dare not for my life,
For you have two big new keen swords
And I have ne'er a knife.

O if I have two new keen swords,
They have cost me deep in my purse,
And you can take the best of them
And I will take the worst.

You can strike the very first blow,
But strike it like a man;
And I will strike the second blow;
I'll kill you if I can.

The very first lick that Matthy Groves struck
He wounded Lord Banner full sore;
The second lick Lord Banner struck
Matthy Groves he spoke no more.

He took her by the lily-white hand,
He laid her on his knee,
Saying: Which do you like the best of the two,
Little Matthy Groves or me?

Very well do I like your red rosy cheeks,
Also your dimpling chin;
Much better do I like little Matthy Groves
Than you and all your kin.

He took her by the lily-white hand,
He led her into the hall.
He drew his sword, cut off her head
And kicked it against the wall.

19 BARBARA ELLEN

O down in Lon - don where I was raised, Down where I got my learn-ing ____ I __ fell in love with a pret-ty lit - tle girl. Her name was __ Bar - b'ry __ El-len.

He courted her for seven long years.
She said she would not have him.
Pretty William went home and took down sick
And sent for Barb'ry Ellen.

He wrote her a letter on his death-bed;
He wrote it slow and moving.
Go take this to my pretty little love
And tell her I am dying.

They took it to his pretty little love;
She read it slow and mourning.
Go take this to my pretty little love
And tell him I am coming.

As she walked on to his bedside,
Says: Young man, young man, you're dying.
He turned his pale face towards the wall
And bursted out a-crying.

He reached his lily-white hand to her.
O come and tell me 'howdey'.
O no, O no, O no, says she,
And she would not go about him.

Do you remember last Saturday night
Down at my father's dwelling,
You passed the drink to the ladies all around
And slighted Barb'ry Ellen.

O yes, I remember last Saturday night
Down at your father's dwelling,
I passed the drink to the ladies all around,
My heart to Barb'ry Ellen.

As she walked down those long stair-steps,
She heard some death-bells ringing,
And every bell it seemed to say:
Hard-hearted Barb'ry Ellen,
Hard-hearted Barb'ry Ellen.*

As she walked down that shady grove
She heard some birds a-singing,
And every bird it seemed to say:
Hard-hearted Barb'ry Ellen,
Hard-hearted Barb'ry Ellen.*

As she walked out the very next day
She saw his corpse a-coming.
O lay him down, O lay him down,
And let me look upon him.

The more she looked the worse she felt,
Till she bursted out a-crying:
I once could have saved pretty William's life,
But I would not go about him.

O mother, O mother, go make my bed,
Go make it soft and narrow.
Pretty William has died for pure, pure love
And I shall die for sorrow.

O father, O father, go dig my grave,
Go dig it deep and narrow;
Pretty William has died for me to-day
And I shall die tomorrow.

A rose grew up from William's grave,
From Barbara Ellen's a brier.
They grew and they grew to the top of the church
Till they could not grow any higher.

They grew and they grew to the top of the church
Till they could not grow any higher;
And there they tied in a true love's knot,
And the rose wrapped round the brier.

* The last two bars of the tune are repeated.

20 LITTLE SON HUGH

(*Sir Hugh*)

As I walked out one ho - li - day Some drops of dew did fall, And

ev - 'ry scho - lar in the school Was out a play - ing ball.

They tossed the ball both to and fro,
To the Jews' garden it flew;
There was none so ready to bring it out
But our little son Hugh.

The Jews' daughter came stepping along
With some apples in her hand,
Saying: Little son Hugh, come go with me
And some apples you may have.

I cannot go, I will not go,
I cannot go at all,
For if my mother were to know,
The red blood she'd make fall.

She took him by the lily-white hand,
She drug him from hall to hall,
And took him to a great stone wall
Where none could hear his call.

She sat him down in a little arm-chair,
And pierced his heart within.
She had a little silver bowl,
His heart's blood she let in.

She took him into the Jews' garden,
The Jews were all asleep;
She threw him into a great deep well,
Was fifty fathoms deep.

His mother broke a birch rod in her hand,
Went walking down the road,
Saying: If I find my little son Hugh,
O I will whip him home.

And when she came to the old Jews' gate,
The Jews were all asleep,
She walked on to a great deep well,
Was fifty fathoms deep.

Saying: Little son Hugh, O are you here,
As I suppose you to be?
O yes, dear mother, I am here
And stand in the need of thee.

With my little penknife pierced through my heart
And the red blood running so free.
O mother, O mother, dig my grave,
Dig it long, wide and deep.

Go bury my Bible at my head,
My prayer book at my feet;
And if any of the scholars ask for me,
Pray tell them I'm asleep.

21 THE DEATH OF QUEEN JANE

Queen Jane was in la – bour Six weeks __ and some more; Her
wo – men grew wear – ied And the mid – wife gave __ o'er.

O women, kind women,
As I take you to be,
Just pierce my right side open
And save my baby.

O no, said her women,
That could never be;
We'll send for King Henry
In the time of your need.

King Henry was sent for
And he bent o'er her bed.
What's the matter with my flower
That her eyes look so red?

O Henry, King Henry,
Pray listen to me,
And pierce my right side open
And save my baby.

O no, said King Henry,
That could never be;
I would lose my sweet flower
To save my baby.

Queen Jane she turned over
And fell in a swound;
And her side was pierced open
And her baby was found.

King Henry fell a-weeping
Till his hands were wrung sore.
The flower of England
Will flourish no more.

So black was the mourning,
So yellow was the bed,
So costly was the white robe
Queen Jane was wrapped in.

The baby was christened
All on the next day;
And its mother's poor body
Lying cold as the clay.

22 GYPSY DAVY

(*The Gypsy Laddie*)

The Squi-re came home late in the night In - quir-ing for his la - dy. The

an - swer that they made to him: She's gone with the gyp- sy Da - vy.

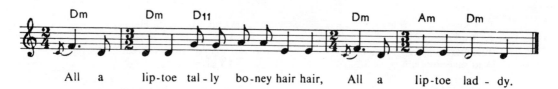

All a lip-toe tal - ly bo-ney hair hair, All a lip-toe lad - dy.

He saddled up his milk-white steed,
He saddled up his pony;
He rode all night till broad daylight
Till he overtook his lady.
    All a lip-toe *etc.*

It's come go back, my dearest dear,
Come back with me, my honey;
I'll swear by the sword that hangs by my side
You never shall want for money.
    All a lip-toe *etc.*

I won't go back, my dearest dear,
I won't go back, my honey,
For I'd rather have a kiss from gypsum's lips
Than all your land and money.
    All a lip-toe *etc.*

Pull off, pull off, your high-heeled shoes
That's made of Spanish leather
And give to me your lily-white hand;
We'll bid farewell for ever.
    All a lip-toe *etc.*

She pulléd off her high-heeled shoes
A-made of Spanish leather
And gave to him her lily-white hand
And bade him farewell for ever.
    All a lip-toe *etc.*

Last night she lay on a soft feather-bed
With her good lord beside her;
To-night she lies on the damp cold ground
With the gypsies all around her.
    All a lip-toe *etc.*

23 THE WIFE WRAPT IN WETHER'S SKIN

There was a man lived in the West, Dan - doo, dan - doo, There

was a man lived in the West, ___ Dan - doo, dan - doo - ah, There

was a man lived in the West Who had a wife that was none of the best. ___

Ram jam ___ gil - li - am ___ dan - doo - ah.

When this old man came in from his plough,
    Dandoo, dandoo,
When this old man came in from his plough,
    Dandoo, dandoo-ah,
When this old man came in from his plough,
Says: Have you got my breakfast now?
    Ram jam gilliam dandoo-ah.

She put a cold slice upon the shelf.
If you want any more you must get it yourself.

The man went out to his sheep-fold
And caught a wether tough and old.

He threw the skin round his wife's back
And that old sheep's hide he did whack.

His wife cried out unto her kin:
He's beating me on my bare skin.

The man he grinned and he replied:
I'm only tanning my old sheep's hide.

24 GEORGIE

(*Geordie*)

As I came ov-er new Lon-don Bridge One mis-ty morn-ing ear - ly, I

o - ver-heard a —— ten-der-hearted girl A - plead-ing for the life of Geor - gie.

Come saddle unto me, my milk-white steed,
The brown one ain't so speedy;
I'll ride away to the king's high court
A-pleading for the life of Georgie.

She rode, she rode to the king's high court
Inquiring for poor Georgie.
Fair lady, you have come too late
For he's condemned already.

It's Georgie never robbed the king's high court,
Nor he never murdered any,
But he stole sixteen of the king's white steeds
And sold them in Virginny.

The king looked over his right shoulder
And this he says to Georgie:
By your own confession you must die.
May the Lord have mercy on thee.

It's Georgie was hung with a silken rope,
Such ropes they are not many;
But Georgie came of a noble race
And was courted by a noble lady.

25 THE HOUSE CARPENTER

(*The Daemon Lover*)

Well met, well met, my own true love, Well met, well met, said he. I've

just returned from the salt, salt sea And it's all for the sake of thee.

O I could have married a king's daughter fair,
I'm sure she'd have married me,
But I refused those golden crowns
And it's all for the sake of thee.

If you could have married a king's daughter fair,
I'm sure you are to blame,
For I am married to a house carpenter,
And I think he's a nice young man.

I pray you leave your house carpenter
And go away with me;
I'll take you where the grass grows green
On the banks of the Aloe Dee.

Have you anything to support me on
To keep me from slavery?
Have you anything to supply my wants
While sailing on the sea?

I have three ships on the ocean wide
A-sailing towards dry land;
Three hundred and sixty sailor men
Shall be at your command.

She took her babe up in her arms
And kisses gave it three.
Saying: Stay at home with your papa dear
And keep him company.

She dressed herself in silk so fine,
Most beautiful to behold.
As she marched down to the brine water side
Bright shone those glittering golds.

She had not been on sea two weeks,
I'm sure it was not three,
Till she lay on the deck of her true lover's boat
And wept most bitterly.

O are you weeping for your gold,
Or is it for your store,
Or is it for your house carpenter
You never shall see any more?

I am not weeping for my gold,
Nor neither for my store.
'Tis all for the love of my darling little babe
I never shall see any more.

She had not been on sea three weeks,
I'm sure it was not four,
Till a leak sprang in her true lover's boat,
And it sank to rise no more.

What banks, what banks before us now
As white as any snow?
Those are the banks of heaven, my love,
Where all good people go.

What banks, what banks before us now
As black as any crow?
Those are the banks of hell, my love,
Where you and I shall go.

26 OUR GOODMAN

O what's this horse a – do-ing here where my horse ought to be? You

old fool, blind fool, can't you ne-ver see? It's no-thing but a milk-cow my

mo-ther sent to me. It's miles I have tra-velled, some for-ty miles or

more; A milk-cow with a sad-dle on I ne-ver saw be-fore.

O what's this coat a-doing here where my coat
   ought to be?
You old fool, blind fool, can't you never see?
It's nothing but a bed-quilt my mother sent to me.
  It's miles I have travelled, some forty miles or
    more;
  A bed-quilt with buttons on I never saw before.

O what are these boots a-doing here where my
   boots ought to be?
You old fool, blind fool, can't you never see?
It's nothing but a cabbage-head my mother sent
   to me.
  It's miles I have travelled, some forty miles or
    more;
  A cabbage-head with boot-heels on I never saw
   before.

O what's this hat a-doing here where my hat
   ought to be?
You old fool, blind fool, can't you never see?
It's nothing but a dish-rag my mother sent to me.
  It's miles I have travelled, some forty miles or
    more,
  A dish-rag with a hat-band on I never saw
   before.

O what are these pants a-doing here where my
   pants ought to be?
You old fool, blind fool, can't you never see?
It's nothing but a petticoat my mother sent to me.
  It's miles I have travelled, some forty miles or
    more,
  A petticoat with gallices* on I never saw before.
  * suspenders

O what's that man a-doing there where I ought
    to be?
You old fool, blind fool, can't you never see?
It's nothing but a baby child my mother sent to me.
    It's miles I have travelled, some forty miles or
    more,
    A baby child with mushtash† on I never saw
    before.

† moustache

27 THE FARMER'S CURST WIFE

There was an old man lived un-der the hill. Sing ti - ro rat-tel-ling day, ___ If he

ain't moved a - way ___ he's liv - ing there still. Sing ti - ro rat-tel - ling day. ___

As this old man went out to his plough,
    Sing tiro rattelling day,
He saw the old devil fly over his mow.
    Sing tiro rattelling day.

The old man cries out: I am undone,
For the devil has come for my oldest son.

It's not your oldest son I crave,
But your damned old scolding wife I'll have.

He took the old woman upon his back
And off he took her all packed in a sack.

He carried her on till he came to hell's gate;
Says: Get down, old lady, right here's the place.

It's twelve little devils came walking by.
Then she up with her foot, kicked eleven in the fire.

The odd little devil peeped over the wall,
Saying: Take her back, daddy, or she'll kill us all.

He humped her up all on his poor back
And away the old fool went walking her back.

The old man was lying there sick in the bed.
With an old pewter pipe she battered his head.

The old man cries out: I am to be cursed;
She's been to hell and come back worse.

28 THE WEEPING WILLOW TREE
(*The Golden Vanity*)

There was   a lit – tle ship   in   the   South A - me – ri – kee,   She

went   by   the   name   of   the   Weep - ing Wil - low Tree,   As   she

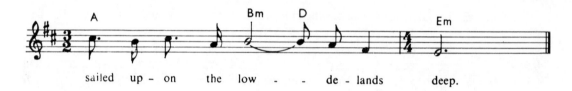

sailed   up – on   the   low –   – de - lands   deep.

There was another ship in the North Amerikee,
She went by the name of the Golden Silveree,
   As she sailed upon the low-de-lands deep.

O captain, O captain, what'll you give to me
If I go and sink the ship of the Weeping Willow
    Tree
   As she sails upon the low-de-lands deep?

O I will give you gold and I'll give to you a fee,
I'll give to you my daughter and married you
    shall be
   As we sail upon the low-de-lands deep.

He bent to his breast and away swam he,
He swam and sank the ship of the Weeping Willow
    Tree
   As she sailed upon the low-de-lands deep.

He bent to his breast and back swam he,
It's back to the ship of the Golden Silveree
   As they sailed upon the low-de-lands deep.

O captain, O captain, O pray take me on board,
For I have been just as good as my word,
   I have sunk her in the low-de-lands deep.

I know that you've been just as good as your word,
But never more will I take you on board
   As we sail upon the low-de-lands deep.

If it wasn't for the love I have for your girl
I'd do unto you as I did unto them.
   I would sink you in the low-de-lands deep.

And he turned upon his back and down went he,
Down, down, down to the bottom of the sea
   As they sailed upon the low-de-lands deep.

29 FAIR SALLY (*The Brown Girl*)

A —— young I - rish la - dy from Lon - don she came, A beau - ti - ful crea - ture, fair Sal - ly by —— name. Her rich - es were more than the —— king did —— pos - sess; Her —— beau - ty was more than her —— wealth at the best.

There was a young squire who livéd right near,
A-courting this lady to make her his dear.
But she was so wealthy, so lofty and high,
That on this young man she would scarce cast an
    eye.

O Sally, O Sally, O Sally, said he,
I fear that your beauty my ruin will be;
Unless that your hatred is turned into love,
I fear that your beauty my ruin will prove.

No hatred for you, sir, nor any other man,
But to say that I love you is more than I can.
So quit your intentions and mend your discourse,
For I never will wed you unless I am forced.

Before six weeks had come or six weeks had passed,
This beautiful creature lay sick at the last.
She sent for this young man she once did deny.
She was pierced to the heart and she knew not for
    why.

O am I the doctor you sent for to come here,
Or am I the young man that loved you so dear?
O you are the doctor can kill or can cure
And without your assistance I'm ruined I'm sure.

O Sally, O Sally, O Sally, said he,
O don't you remember that you once courted me?
I courted for love, you slighted with scorn.
Now I will reward you for what you have done.

For what's passed and done, sir, forget and forgive
And grant me assistance some longer to live.
I'll ne'er do that, Sally, while I do draw breath,
But I'll dance on your grave when you're laid in
    the earth.

Then off of her fingers pulled diamond rings three,
Saying: Take these and wear them when dancing
    on me.
I'll freely forgive you although you won't forgive me.
Ten thousand times over my folly I see.

30 THE LADY AND THE DRAGOON

There was a lit - tle sol - dier just late - ly come from war. He

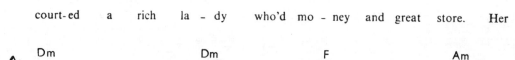

court-ed a rich la - dy who'd mo - ney and great store. Her

rich - es were so great,— they scarce - ly could be told,— But

yet she loved the sol – dier be – cause he was so bold.

She says: My little soldier, I would freely be your wife,
But I know my cruel old father would surely take your life.
He drew his sword and pistol and hung them by his side
And swore he would get married and let what would betide.

And when they had got married and returning home again,
Out slipped her cruel old father and seven arméd men,
Saying: Since you are determined to be the soldier's wife,
Down in some lonesome valley I'll shortly take his life.

O, says the little soldier, no time there is to tattle,
For I have just been married and am in no fix for battle.
But he drew his sword and pistol and causéd them for to rattle.
The lady held the horses while the soldier fought the battle.

The first one that he came to he ran him through the main,
The next one that he came to he servéd him the same.
Let's run, let's run, said the others, or else we'll all be slain,
For to fight the valiant soldier we see 'tis all in vain.

Up steps her cruel old father, a-speaking mighty
    bold:
O you shall have my daughter and a thousand
    pound of gold.
Fight on, fight on, says the lady, the pile it is too
    small.
O stop, says the old man, and you shall have it all.

31 LOCKS AND BOLTS

Come men and maids and lis-ten a-while; I'll tell you a-bout my— dar-ling. She's the lit-tle one I— love— so well; She's al-most the com-plete one.

Her yellow hair like glittering gold
Comes jingling down her pillow.
She's the little one I love so well;
She's like the weeping willow.

I went unto her uncle's house
Inquiring for my darling.
The answer was: She is not here;
I've no such in my keeping.

But when she heard my lonely voice
She answered at the window,
Saying: I would be with you soon, my love,
But locks and bolts do hinder.

I stood for a moment all in a maze;
I viewed her long and tenderly;
My passion flew, my sword I drew;
I swore that house I'd enter.

I took my sword in my right hand
And my love all in the other.
Come all young men that love like me,
Fight on till you gain your lover.

32 JACK WENT A-SAILING

Jack went a - sail - ing With trou-ble on his mind, To leave his na - tive coun - try And his dar - ling dear be - hind. Sing— ree and sing low, So ____ fare you well, my dear.

She dressed herself in men's array
And apparel she put on;
Unto the field of battle
She marched her men along.
  Sing ree and sing low,
  So fàre you well, my dear.

Your cheeks too red and rosy,
Your fingers too neat and small,
And your waist too slim and slender
To face a cannon ball.

My cheeks are red and rosy,
My fingers neat and small,
But it never makes me tremble
To face a cannon ball.

The battle being ended,
She rode the circle round
And through the dead and dying
Her darling dear she found.

She picked him up all in her arms,
She carried him down to town,
And sent for a London doctor
To heal his bleeding wounds.

This couple they got married,
So well they did agree;
This couple they got married,
And why not you and me?

33 WILLIAM HALL

I'll tell you of a brisk young farm-er Who is a cred-it to a-ny man. He____ court-ed a fair and a hand-some la-dy Who did dwell in__ Shel-vey Town.

When her old parents came to know this
They grew angry and did say:
We'll send him over and over the ocean,
Where his face you'll no more see.

He sailed and he sailed all over the ocean
Till he came to his own sea-side.
If Molly is alive and I can find her
I'll make her my lawful bride.

As he was a-walking, as he was a-talking,
As he was a-walking up the street,
Cold drops of rain fell just as it happened
I and my true love did meet.

How do you do, my pretty fair lady,
Now do you think you can fancy me?
No, No, kind sir, and it was her answer,
My true love is across the sea.

O describe your own true lover,
O describe him unto me.
Perhaps I saw some sword run through him,
For I've just returned from sea.

O I can describe my own true lover,
He is proper, neat and tall;
He has black hair and he wears it curly;
O his pretty blue eyes beat all.

O yes, I saw a ball go through him,
O he's dead, I saw him fall;
He had black hair and he wore it curly
And his name was William Hall.

O love is great and love is charming
When we have it in our view;
But now we are parted and broken-hearted.
O good Lord, what shall I do?

Cheer up, cheer up, my pretty fair lady,
Cheer up, cheer up, for I am he;
And for to convince you of this matter,
Here is a ring that you gave me.

They joined their loving hands together,
Down to the church-house they did go
For to get married to each other,
Whether their parents were willing or no.

34 WILLIAM AND POLLY
(*Lisbon*)

Sweet Wil-liam went to Pol - ly To give her to un - der - stand That he had to go and leave — her To go to a fo - reign land. —

O stay at home, Sweet William,
O stay at home, said she,
O stay at home, Sweet William,
And do not go to sea.

My king doth give command, my love,
And I am bound to go;
And if it were to save my life
I dare not answer No.

My yellow hair I will cut off,
Men's clothing I'll put on;
Like a true and faithful servant
It's you I'll wait upon.

The men do lie a-bleeding there,
The bullets swiftly fly,
And the silver trumpets a-sounding
To drown the dismal cry.

O tell me not of danger,
For God will be my guide;
And I value not no danger
When William's by my side.

O Polly, dearest Polly,
These words have gained my heart,
And we will have a wedding
Before we ever part.

This couple they got married
And William's gone to sea
And Polly she's a-waiting
All in their own country.

For specimen guitar accompaniment see page 16

35 SWEET WILLIAM

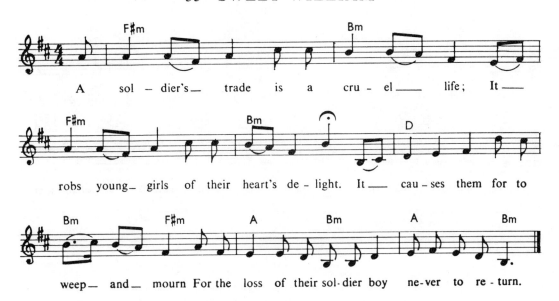

A sol – dier's — trade is a cru – el — life; It —
robs young — girls of their heart's de – light. It — cau – ses them for to
weep — and — mourn For the loss of their sol-dier boy ne-ver to re - turn.

O father, O father build me a boat
That over the ocean I may float
And every ship that I pass by
I will inquire for my sweet soldier boy.

O captain, O captain, tell me true,
Does my sweet soldier boy sail with you?
O answer me quick and that will give me joy,
For I never loved any but my sweet soldier boy.

O lady, O lady, he is not here,
For he got killed in the battle, my dear.
At the head of Rocky Island as we passed by
There we did see your sailor boy lie.

Go dig my grave both wide and deep,
A marble stone at my head and feet.
Upon my breast there'll come a turtle dove
To show the world that I died of love.

36 THE CRUEL SHIP'S CARPENTER

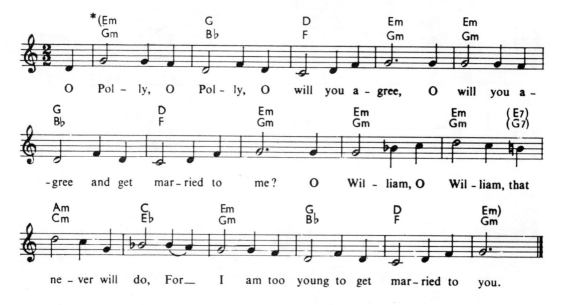

O Pol - ly, O Pol - ly, O will you a - gree, O will you a -gree and get mar - ried to me? O Wil - liam, O Wil - liam, that ne - ver will do, For__ I am too young to get mar - ried to you.

O Polly, O Polly, if you will agree,
before we get married some pleasure we'll see.
He led her over mountains and valleys so deep
Till at length pretty Polly began for to weep.

O William, O William, you're leading me astray
On purpose my innocent heart to betray.
O Polly, O Polly, I guess you spoke right,
I was digging your grave the best part of last night.

She fold' her arms around him without any fear.
How can you bear to kill the girl that loves you so
 dear?
O Polly, O Polly, we've no time to stand.
And instantly drew a short knife in his hand.

He piercéd her heart and the blood it did flow,
And into her grave her fair body did throw.
He covered her up and away he did go.
He left nothing but small birds to make their sad
 moan.

He entered his ship upon the salt sea so wide
And swore by his Maker he'd sail to the other side.
Whilst he was a-sailing in his full heart's content
The ship sprung a leak, to the bottom she went.

Whilst he was a-lying there all in his sad surprise
He saw pretty Polly appear before his eyes.
O William, O William, you've no time to stay;
There's a debt to the devil that you're bound to
 pay.

* Alternative guitar chords with capo at 3rd fret.

37 THE TRUE LOVER'S FAREWELL

O fare you well, my own true love, O fare you well for a while; I'm
go-ing a-way but I'll come a-gain If I go __ ten thou-sand mile.

The crow that is so black, my love,
Will surely turn to white
And if ever I prove false to the girl I love
Bright day shall turn to night.

Bright day shall turn to night, my love,
And the rocks shall melt with the sun
And the fire will freeze and be no more
And the raging sea will burn.

O don't you see yon little turtle dove
A-skipping from vine to vine,
A-mourning the loss of its own true love
Just as I mourn for mine?

So fare you well, my own true love,
So fare you well for a while;
I'm going away, but I'm coming again
If I go ten thousand mile.

38 THE CUCKOO

The cu-ckoo __ is a pret-ty bird, She sings as __ she __ flies, She
brings us _____ glad_ tid - ings And_ tells us no __ lies.

She sucks all sweet flowers
For to make her voice clear
And she never hollers Cuckoo
Till the summer is near.

It's meeting it is a pleasure
And parting it is a grief;
And a false-hearted true lover
Is worse than a thief.

They'll hug you, they'll kiss you,
They'll tell you more lies
Than the green leaves on the willow
Or the stars in the skies.

O the cuckoo is a pretty bird,
She sings as she flies,
She brings us glad tidings
And tells us no lies.

61

39 PRETTY SARO

I— came to— this— coun-try in — eight-een for-ty – nine, I—
saw so ma-ny lo - vers, but I ne – ver saw mine. I—
viewed all a— round me and— saw I was a - lone And
me a poor stran - ger and— far from my home.

I wish I were a poet and could write a fine hand;
I would write my love a letter that she might
    understand;
I would send it by the waters where the island
    overflows.
I'll think on pretty Saro wherever I go.

I wish I were a small bird, had wings and could
    fly;
Right to my love's dwelling this night I'd draw
    nigh;
In her lily-white arms all night I would lie
And out some small window next morning I'd fly.

40 MY DEAREST DEAR

My dear-est dear, the time draws near When I and you must part; And no one knows the in-ner grief of my poor ach-ing heart, Or what I suf-fer for your sake, For the one I love so dear. I wish that I could go with you, Or you could tar-ry here.

I wish your breast were made of glass
And in't I might behold;
Your name in secret I would write
In letters of bright gold.
Your name in secret I would write,
Pray believe me what I say;
You are the man that I'll love best
Unto my dying day.

But when you're on some distant shore,
Think on your absent friend.
And when the wind blows high and clear
A line or two pray send;
And when the wind blows high and clear
Pray send it, love to me,
That I may know by your hand-write
How times have gone with thee.

For specimen guitar accompaniment see page 16

41 BLACK IS THE COLOUR

But black is the co-lour of my true love's hair. His face is like some ro-sy fair; The pret-tiest face and the neat-est hands. I love the ground —— where-on he stands.

I love my love and well he knows
I love the ground whereon he goes.
If you no more on earth I see,
I can't serve you as you have me.

The winter's past and the leaves are green,
The time is past that we have seen;
But still I hope the time will come
When you and I shall be as one.

I go to the Clyde for to mourn and weep,
But satisfied I never could sleep.
I'll write to you in a few short lines;
I'll suffer death ten thousand times.

My own true love, so fare you well,
The time has passed but I wish you well;
But still I hope the time will come
When you and I will be as one.

I love my love and well he knows
I love the ground whereon he goes.
The prettiest face, the neatest hands.
I love the ground whereon he stands.

42 THE FALSE YOUNG MAN

Come in, come in, my— old true love, And— chat a-while ———— with me, For it's been three — quarters of one long— year or more Since I spoke one — word — to — thee.

I can't come in, nor I shan't sit down,
For I haven't a moment of time.
Since you are engaged with another true love
Your heart is no more mine.

When your heart was mine, my old true love,
And you head lay on my breast,
You could make me believe by the falling of your
   arm
That the sun rose up in the West.

There's many a girl that can go all round about
And hear the small birds sing,
And many a girl that stays at home alone
And rocks the cradle and spins.

There's many a star that shall jingle in the West,
There's many a leaf below,
There's many a damn will light upon a man
For serving a poor girl so.

43 THE DEAR COMPANION

I once did have a dear com-pan-ion, In-deed I
thought his love— my own Un-til a black-eyed girl be-
-trayed me And then he cares no— more for me.

Just go and leave me if you wish to,
It will never trouble me,
For in your heart you love another
And in my grave I'd rather be.

Last night you were sweetly sleeping,
Dreaming in some sweet repose,
While I, a poor girl, broken, broken-hearted,
Listen to the wind that blows.

When I see your babe a-laughing
It makes me think of your sweet face,
But when I see your babe a-crying
It makes me think of my disgrace.

44 THE IRISH GIRL

As I walked out one May morning Down by the ri-ver-side I
cast my— eyes a—round me And an I-rish— girl I spied.

Her cheeks were red and rosy
And coal-black was her hair.
How costly were the jewels
That Irish girl did wear.

As I walked out that May morning
My true love passing by,
I knew her mind was changing
By the movement of her eyes.

O don't you now remember, love,
When you gave me your right hand,
You vowed if you got married
That I should be the man.

I wish I were a butterfly,
I'd fly to my love's nest;
I wish I were a linnet,
I'd sing my love to rest.

I wish I were a nightingale,
I'd sing to the morning clear;
I'd hold you in my arms, my love,
The girl I love so dear.

45 COME ALL YOU FAIR AND TENDER LADIES

Come all you fair and ten-der la-dies, Take warn-ing how you_ court_ young men; They're like bright stars of a sum-mer's morn-ing, They'll first ap-pear and_ then be gone.

They'll tell to you some loving story,
They will declare their love is true;
Straightway they'll go and court some other
And that's the love they have for you.

If I had known before I courted
That love had been so hard to win
I'd have locked my heart in a box of golden
And a-fastened it up with a silver pin.

I wish I were a little sparrow,
Or some of those that fly so high,
I'd fly away to my false lover
And when he'd talk I would be nigh.

But as it is, I am no sparrow
And neither have I wings to fly.
I'll sit down here in grief and sorrow,
I'll weep and pass my troubles by.

46 ARISE! ARISE!

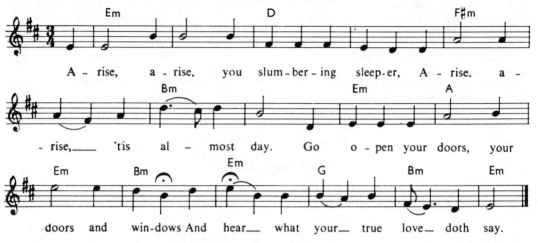

A - rise, a - rise, you slum-ber-ing sleep-er, A - rise, a - rise,___ 'tis al - most day. Go o - pen your doors, your doors and win-dows And hear___ what your___ true love___ doth say.

O who is this that knocks at my window,
That speaks my name so familiarly?
'Tis James, 'tis James, your own true lover
That wants to speak one word to thee.

Go away from my window, you'll waken my
    father;
He's lying now a-taking his rest,
And in his hand he holds a weapon
To kill the one that my heart loves best.

Go away from my window, you'll waken my
    mother;
Such tales of love she scorns to hear.
You'd better go court, go court some other,
She kindly whispered in my ear.

I won't go court, go court some other,
By what I say I mean no harm.
I want to win you from your mother
And rest you in a true love's arms.

O down in yon valley there grows a green willow;
I wish it were across my breast.
It might·cut off all grief and sorrow
And set my troubled mind at rest.

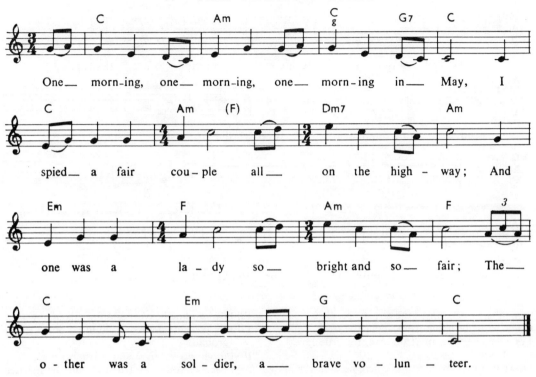

One— morn-ing, one— morn-ing, one— morn-ing in— May, I
spied— a fair cou-ple all— on the high-way; And
one was a la-dy so— bright and so— fair; The—
o-ther was a sol-dier, a— brave vo-lun-teer.

Good-morning, good-morning, good-morning to
  thee.
Now where are you going, my pretty lady?
I'm going to travel to the banks of the sea
To see the waters gliding, hear the nightingales
  sing.

They hadn't been there but an hour or two
Till out of his knapsack his fiddle he drew.
The tune that he played caused the valleys to ring.
O hearken, says the lady, how the nightingales
  sing.

Pretty lady, pretty lady, 'tis time to give o'er.
O no, pretty soldier, please play one tune more.
I'd rather hear your fiddle one touch of the string
Than see the waters gliding, hear the nightingales
  sing.

Pretty soldier, pretty soldier, will you marry me?
O no, pretty lady that never can be.
I've a wife back in London and children twice
  three.
Two wives in the army is too many for me.

48 GREEN BUSHES

As I was a-walk-ing one morn-ing in the Spring, I spied a fair dam-sel, so sweet-ly did she sing. O yon-der comes my true love, my true love I do see Down by those green bush-es where he thinks he'll meet me.

Come let us be going, kind sir, if you please,
Come let us be going from under the trees.
For yonder comes my true love, my true love I
  do see
Down by those green bushes where he thinks he'll
  meet me.

O when he came there and he found she was gone
He stood like some lamkin that was all forlorn.
She's gone with some other, she's quite forsaken
  me
Down among the green bushes where she thinks
  to meet me.

I'll buy you fine beavers and fine silken gowns,
I'll buy you fine petticoats flounced down to the
  ground.
If you will prove loyal and constant to me
And forsake your own true love and get married
  to me.

I don't want your beavers nor fine silken hose,
I was never so hard run as to marry for clothes;
But if you will prove loyal and constant to me
I'll forsake my own true love and get married to
  thee.

I'll be like some school-boy, and spend my time
  at play;
No false-hearted lady will be-lead me astray.
She's gone with some other which grieves me full
  sore,
So adieu to green bushes; 'tis time to give o'er.

49 GOOD-MORNING MY PRETTY LITTLE MISS

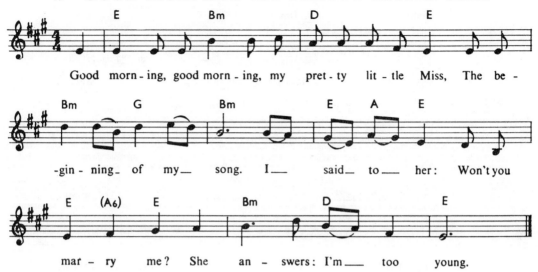

Good morn-ing, good morn-ing, my pret-ty lit-tle Miss, The be-

-gin-ning_ of my_ song. I_ said_ to _ her: Won't you

mar-ry me? She an-swers: I'm _ too young.

The younger you are the better for me,
More fitting to be my bride.
He courted her by compliment
Till he got her to comply.

The night has passed and the day has come,
The morning sun does shine.
O I will arise, put on my clothes
And then, sweet love, I'm gone.

O that is not what you promised me
All down by the greenwood side.
You promised for to marry me
And make me your sweet bride.

If ever I promised to marry you
It was all in a merry mood,
For I will avow and I will swear
I never was born for you.

O girls can go to market town,
Go dressed so neat and fine,
While I a poor girl must stay at home
And rock the cradle and spin.

There is a herb in father's garden
And some they call it rue.
The fish will dive, the swallow fly,
But a man will never be true.

50 THE REBEL SOLDIER

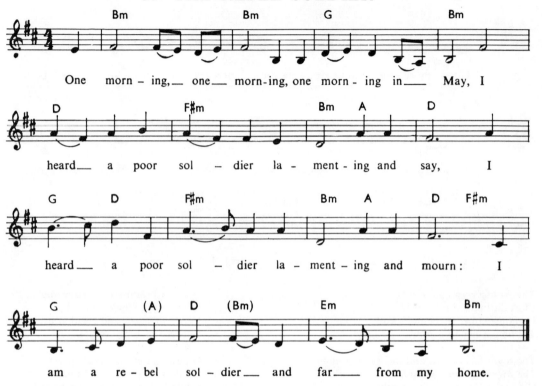

One morn-ing,— one— morn-ing, one morn-ing in— May, I heard— a poor sol – dier la - ment-ing and say, I heard — a poor sol – dier la – ment – ing and mourn: I am a re - bel sol – dier— and far— from my home.

It's grape-shot and musket and the cannons lumber loud.
There's a many a mangled body, a blanket for their shroud,
There's a many a mangled body left on the field alone.
I am a rebel soldier and far from my home.

I'll eat when I'm hungry and drink when I am dry.
If the Yankees don't kill me I'll live until I die,
If the Yankees don't kill me and cause me to mourn.
I am a rebel soldier and far from my home.

I'll build me a castle on some green mountain high
Where the wild geese can see me as they do pass me by,
Where the wild geese can see and hear my sad mourn.
I am a rebel soldier and far from my home.

51 THE RICH OLD LADY

There was a rich old la – dy In Lon-don she did dwell; She
loved her own man dear – ly, But an – o-ther man twice as well.

Sing to the I – ree - O, ____ Sing to the I – ree - O.

O she went to the doctor's shop
As hard as she could go,
To see if anything she could find
To make her old man blind.
    Sing to the I-ree-O,
    Sing to the I-ree-O.

She got two walloping mar'-bones,*
She made him eat them all.
He says: O my dear beloved wife,
I can't see you at all.

If I could see my way to go,
I'd go to the river and drown.
She says: I'll go along with you
For fear you go astray.

O she got up behind him
Just ready for to plunge him in.
He stepped a little to one side
And headlong she went in.

O she began to kick and scream
As loud as she could bawl.
He said: O my dear beloved wife,
I can't see you at all.

He being tender-hearted
And thinking she could swim,
He got him a great long pole
And pushed her further in.

* marrow-bones

52 KATIE MOREY

Come young, come old, come all draw nigh, Come lis-ten to my sto-ry. I'll tell you of a plan I've made To fool Miss Ka-tie Mo-rey. My too-i-ree I - O, ⸺ My too-i-ree I - O.

I went unto her father's house
Just like a clever fellow.
I told her that the plums were ripe,
Yes, they were fine and mellow.
    My too-i-ree I-O,
    My too-i-ree I-O.

She says: My dear, my dearest dear,
There's something to betray us;
My father dear is on his way
And he'll be sure to see us.

But if the highest tree you'd climb
Till he gets out of sight, sir,
It's then we'll go to yonders grove
And spend one happy hour.

The tree was rough, he climbed so tough
And on the top he stopped, sir,
At every jerk he tore his shirt
And on the top he stopped, sir.

As she went trippling over the plain,
She looked so neat and active.
And there he sat on the top of the tree
All raving and distracted.

53 I MUST AND I WILL GET MARRIED

One morn - ing, one morn - ing, the wea - ther be - ing fair, The

mo - ther and the daugh - ter walked out to take the air; And

as they were a - walk - ing this maid be - gan to vow: I

must and I will get mar - ried, I'm in the no - tion now.

O daughter, O daughter, 'tis hold your foolish tongue.
What makes you want to marry? You know you are too young.
I'm sixteen now, dear mother, and that you must allow.
I must and I will get married, I'm in the notion now.

Suppose you were to try, my dear, and could not find a man?
O never mind, dear mother, for there is Miller Sam.
He calls me his milk and honey, goes milking of my cow.
I must and I will get married, I'm in the notion now.

Suppose he were to fool with you as he has done before?
O never mind, dear mother, for there are plenty more;
For there is Jack the farmer goes whistling to his plough.
I must and I will get married, I'm in the notion now.

54 OLD WOMAN

(*The Deaf Woman's Courtship*)

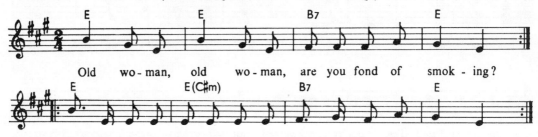

Old wo-man, old wo-man, are you fond of smok-ing?

Speak a lit-tle loud-er, sir, I'm ra-ther hard of hear-ing.

Old woman, old woman, are you fond of carding?
Speak a little louder, sir, I'm rather hard of hearing.

Old woman, old woman, will you let me court you?
Speak a little louder, sir, I just begin to hear you.

Old woman, old woman, don't you want to marry me?
Lord have mercy on my soul, I think that now I hear you.

55 COME MY LITTLE ROVING SAILOR

Come my lit-tle rov-ing sai-lor, Come my lit-tle rov-ing bee,— Come my

lit-tle rov-ing sai-lor, Come sai-lor boy, won't you mar-ry me?

Madam, I have gold and silver,
Madam, I have house and land,
Madam, I have a world of treasure,
All shall be at your command.

What care I for your gold and silver?
What care I for your house and land?
What care I for a world of treasure?
All I want is a handsome man.

Madam, do not stand on beauty,
Beauty is a fading flower;
The reddest rose in yonder garden
Will fade away in half an hour.

56 THE MILLER'S WILL

There was an old mil - ler by ev'-ry-one known, He had three sons was

all nigh grown. When he came to die and make his will He had nothing to give but an

old tub-mill. Tra-la-la-la-la, tra-la-la-la, tra-la-la-la-lee.

> He first called up his oldest son.
> He says: My son, I'm almost done.
> And if the mill to you I'd make,
> Pray tell me how much toll you intend to take?
> Tra-la-la-la-la, tra-la-la-la, tra-la-la-la-lee.

O dear father, my name is Heck,
And out of every bushel I'll take one peck;
And every bushel I do grind,
A very fine living at that I'll find.

You are a fool, the old man said,
You have not fairly learned my trade.
The mill to you I will not give,
For never a miller at that can live.

He next called up his second son.
He says: My son, I'm almost done.
And if the mill to you I'd make,
Pray tell me how much toll you intend to take?

O dear father, my name is Ralph,
And out of every bushel I'll take one half;
And every bushel I do grind,
A very fine living at that I'll find.

You are a fool, the old man said,
You have not fairly learned my trade.
The mill to you I will not give,
For never a miller at that can live.

He next called up his youngest son.
He says: My son, I'm almost done.
And if the mill to you I'd make,
Pray tell me how much toll you intend to take?

O dear father, I am your son,
I'll take three pecks and leave just one.
And if a good living at that I do lack,
I'll take the other and swear to the sack.

You are my son, the old man said,
For you have fairly learned my trade.
The mill is yours, the old man cried.
And then he closed up his eyes and died.

57 BETTY ANNE

Lor, lor, my lit-tle Bet-ty Anne, Lor, lor, I say,

Lor, lor, my lit-tle Bet-ty Anne, I'm going a-way to stay.

Her cheeks as red as a red, red rose, Her eyes as a diamond brown.

Go-ing to see my pret-ty lit-tle Miss Be-fore the sun goes down.

Lor, lor, my little Betty Anne, *etc.*
The rings upon my true love's hands,
They shine so bright like gold.
Going to see my pretty little Miss
Before it rains or snows.

Lor, lor, my little Betty Anne, *etc.*
When I am up at the field at work
Then I sit down and cry,
Studying about my blue-eyed boy,
I thought to my God I'd die.

Lor, lor, my little Betty Anne, *etc.*
O fly around, my pretty little Miss,
O fly around I say,
Fly around, my pretty little Miss,
You'll almost drive me crazy.

Lor, lor, my little Betty Anne, *etc.*
O fly around, my pretty little Miss,
O fly around my dandy,
Fly around, my pretty little Miss.
I don't want no more of your candy.

58 THE TREE IN THE WOOD

There was a lit-tle oak in yon-ders field, The prettiest lit-tle oak I

e - ver did see. O, O, the oak in the ground And the

green leaves grew all a - round and a-round And the green leaves grew all a - round.

And on that oak there was a limb,
The prettiest little limb I ever did see.
O, O, the limb on the oak
And the oak in the ground
   And the green leaves grew all around and
   around
   And the green leaves grew all around.

And on that limb there was a twig,
The prettiest little twig I ever did see,
The twig on the limb, *etc.*

And on that twig there was a nest, *etc.*

And in that nest there was an egg, *etc.*

And in that egg there was a bird, *etc.*

And on that bird there was a down, *etc.*

And on that down there was a feather,
The prettiest little feather I ever did see.
O, O, the feather on the down
And the down on the bird
And the bird in the egg
And in the egg in the nest
And the nest on the twig
And the twig on the limb
And the limb on the oak
And the oak in the ground
   And the green leaves grew all around and
   around
   And the green leaves grew all around.

   * This bar is sung twice in the second verse, three
   times in the third and so on.
     When this bar is repeated, guitarists can play Em
   and C alternately.

59 THE RIDDLE SONG

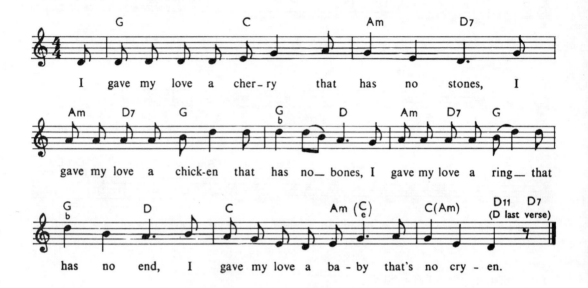

How can there be a cherry that has no stones?
How can there be a chicken that has no bones?
How can there be a ring that has no end?
How can there be a baby that's no cry-en?

A cherry when it's blooming it has no stones,
A chicken when it's pipping it has no bones,
A ring when it's rolling it has no end,
A baby when it's sleeping there's no cry-en.

60 WHEN ADAM WAS CREATED

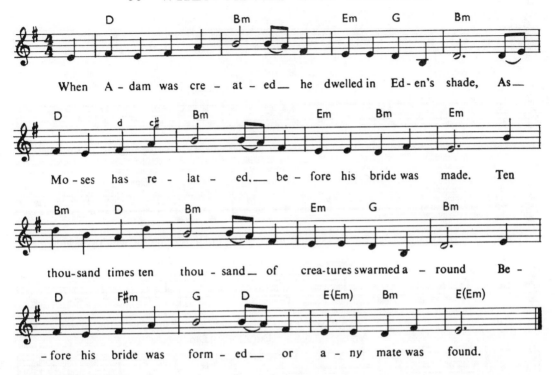

When A-dam was cre-at-ed— he dwelled in Ed-en's shade, As—
Mo-ses has re-lat-ed,— be-fore his bride was made. Ten
thou-sand times ten thou-sand— of crea-tures swarmed a-round Be-
-fore his bride was form-ed— or a-ny mate was found.

He had no conversation, he seemed like one alone,
Then to his admiration he found he'd lost a bone.
Great was his exaltation when first he saw his bride,
Great was his elevation to see her by his side.

This woman was not taken from Adam's head,
    we know,
And she must not rule over him, 'tis evidently so.
This woman was not taken from Adam's feet,
    we see,
And he must not abuse her, the meaning seems
    to be.

This woman she was taken from under Adam's
    arms
And she must be protected from hunger and from
    harm.
This woman she was taken from near to Adam's
    heart,
By this we are directed that they must never part.

To you, most loving bridegroom, to you, most
    loving bride,
Be sure you live as Christians and for your house
    provide.
Avoid all discontent and don't sow the seeds of
    strife,
As is the solemn duty of every man and wife.

61 SINNER MAN

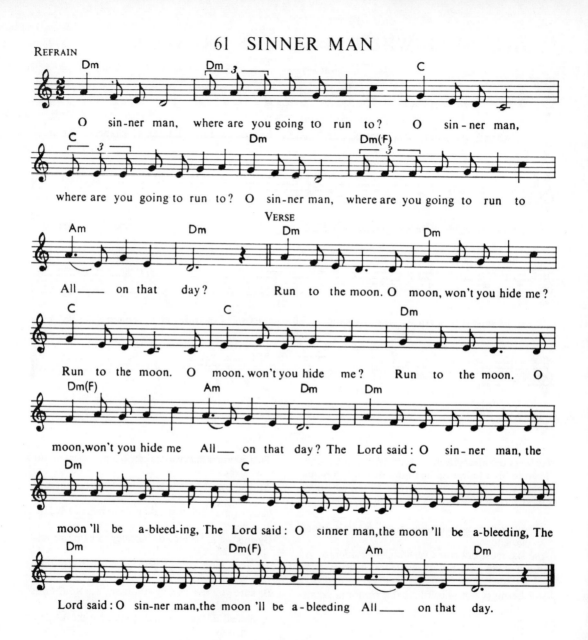

O sinner man, where are you going to run to?
   (*3 times*)
All on that day.
Run to the stars. O stars won't you hide me? *Etc.*
The Lord said: O sinner man, the stars'll be
   a-falling. *Etc.*

O sinner man, *etc.*
Run to the sea. O sea, won't you hide me? *Etc.*
The Lord said: O sinner man, the sea'll be
   a-sinking. *Etc.*

O sinner man, *etc.*
Run to the Lord. O Lord, won't you hide me? *Etc.*
The Lord said: O sinner man, you ought to've
   been a-praying. *Etc.*

O sinner man, *etc.*
Run to Satan. O Satan won't you hide me? *Etc.*
Satan said: O sinner man, step right in (*3 times*)
   All on that day.

62 THE CROW-FISH MAN

Wake up! dar-ling, don't sleep too— late, The crow – fish man's done

passed our gate This morn-ing——— so soon.

Selling crow-fish two for a dime,
Nobody's crow-fish eats like mine
   This morning so soon.

Around the mountains I must go.
If anything happens let me know
   This morning so soon.

Wake up! darling, don't sleep too late,
The crow-fish man's done passed our gate
   This morning so soon.

63 SALLY ANNE

O where are you go - ing, Sal - ly Anne? O where are you go - ing,

Sal - ly Anne? O where are you go - ing, Sal - ly Anne? I'm

go - ing to the wed - ding, Sal - ly Anne. O shake that lit - tle foot,

Sal - ly Anne, O shake that lit - tle foot, Sal - ly Anne, O shake that lit - tle foot,

Sal - ly Anne, You're a pret - ty good dan - cer, Sal - ly Anne.

64 CRIPPLE CREEK

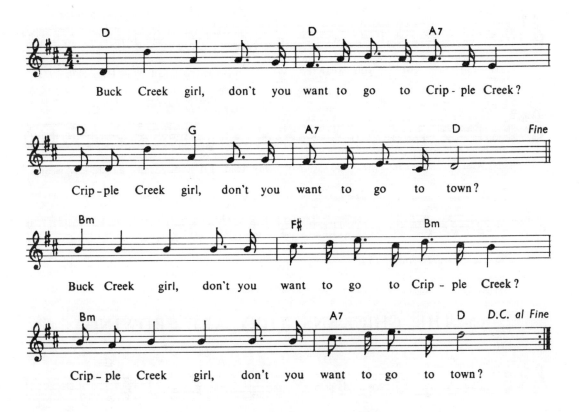

Buck Creek girl, don't you want to go to Crip-ple Creek?

Crip-ple Creek girl, don't you want to go to town?

Buck Creek girl, don't you want to go to Crip-ple Creek?

Crip-ple Creek girl, don't you want to go to town?

Alternative version

Buck Creek girls, don't you want to go to Somerset?
Somerset girls, don't you want to go to town?

65 WILL YOU WEAR RED?

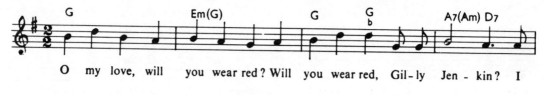

O my love, will you wear red? Will you wear red, Gil-ly Jen-kin? I

won't wear red, for it's the co-lour of my head. I'll buy me a dil-low, wear a

dou-ble o-ver dill, I'll buy me a dil-low, wear a dai-sy.

66 THE CHICKENS THEY ARE CROWING

The chick-ens they are crow — ing, a - crow - ing, a - crow-ing, The

chick-ens they are crow - ing, for it is al-most day — light.

My mother she will scold me, will scold me, will scold me,
My mother she will scold me for staying away all night.

My father he'll uphold me, uphold me, uphold me,
My father he'll uphold me and say I've done just right.

I won't go home till morning, till morning, till morning.
I won't go home till morning and I'll stay with the girls all night.

The chickens they are crowing, a-crowing, a-crowing,
The chickens they are crowing, for it is almost daylight.

67 GOING TO BOSTON

Good-bye, girls, I'm going to Bos-ton, Good-bye, girls, I'm going to Bos-ton,

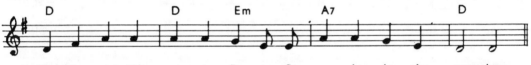

Good-bye, girls, I'm going to Bos-ton So ear-ly in the morn-ing.

Rights and lefts and play the bet-ter, Rights and lefts and play the bet-ter,

Rights and lefts and play the bet-ter So ear-ly in the morn-ing.

O ain't you pretty in the ball-room (*3 times*)
So early in the morning.
Swing your partners and you'll get her (*3 times*)
So early in the morning.

Now we'll promenade one, two, three (*3 times*)
So early in the morning
Needle in the haystack O (*3 times*)
So early in the morning.

68 SOLDIER BOY FOR ME

We go walk – ing on the green grass, Thus, thus, thus. Come

all you pret – ty fair maids, Come walk a – long with us. So

pret – ty and so fair As you take your-self to be, I'll

choose you for a part – ner. Come walk a – long with me.

I would not marry a blacksmith;
He smuts his nose and chin.
I'd rather marry a soldier boy
That marches through the wind.
O soldier boy, O soldier boy,
O soldier boy for me.
If ever I get married
A soldier's wife I'll be.

I would not marry a doctor;
He's always killing the sick
I'd rather marry a soldier boy
That marches double quick.
O soldier boy, O soldier boy,
O soldier boy for me.
If ever I get married
A soldier's wife I'll be.

I would not marry a farmer;
He's always selling grain.
I'd rather marry a soldier boy
That marches through the rain.
O soldier boy, O soldier boy,
O soldier boy for me.
If ever I get married
A soldier's wife I'll be.

We go walking up the green grass,
Thus, thus, thus.
Come all you pretty fair maids,
Come walk along with us.
So pretty and so fair
As you take yourself to be,
I'll choose you for a partner.
Come walk along with me.

69 NOTTAMUN TOWN

In Not-ta-mun Town__ not a soul would look up,__ Not a soul would look

up,__ not a soul would look down,__ Not a soul would look up,__ not a soul would look

down__ To tell me the way__ to Not - ta - mun Town.__

I rode a big horse that was called a grey mare,
Grey mane and tail, grey stripes down his back,
Grey mane and tail, grey stripes down his back,
There wasn't a hair on him but what was called
    black.

She stood so still, she threw me to the dirt,
She tore my hide and bruised my shirt;
From stirrup to stirrup I mounted again
And on my ten toes I rode over the plain.

Met the King and the Queen and a company of
    men
A-walking behind and a-riding before.
A stark naked drummer came walking along
With his hands in his bosom a-beating his drum.

Sat down on a hot and cold frozen stone,
Ten thousand stood round me yet I was alone.
Took my heart in my hand to keep my head warm.
Ten thousand got drowned that never was born.

For specimen guitar accompaniment see page 18

70 THE SALLY BUCK

I start-ed out a - hunt - ing One cold and win - ter day, The leaves they were a - grow - ing green And the flowers were fresh and gay, gay, And the flowers were fresh and gay.

I tracked the Sally buck all day,
I tracked him through the snow,
I tracked him through the waterside
And under he did go, go,
And under he did go.

I loaded up my pistols
And under water went,
To kill the fattest buck, sir,
It was my whole intent, intent,
It was my whole intent.

I got under the water
Ten thousand feet or more;
I fired off my pistols,
Like cannons they did roar, roar,
Like cannons they did roar.

Out of ten and twenty big fat bucks,
By chance I killéd one.
The rest they raised their bristles
And at me they did come, come,
And at me they did come.

Some they were on top of me,
A-holding of me down;
Ten and twenty big fat bucks
They pinned me to the ground, ground,
They pinned me to the ground.

My hide was like a riddle
That a bull-dog could jump through;
And this it made me angry
And my broad sword I drew, drew,
And my broad sword I drew.

I bent my gun a circle,
I fired around the hill,
And out of ten and twenty bucks
Ten thousand did I kill, kill,
Ten thousand did I kill.

To the stars I sold my venison,
To the moon I sold my skins,
I took the rest to the forfeit barn
And it would not all go in, in,
And it would not all go in.

71 I WHIPPED MY HORSE

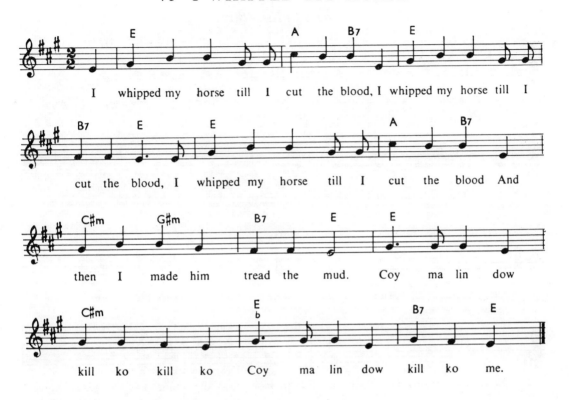

I whipped my horse till I cut the blood, I whipped my horse till I cut the blood, I whipped my horse till I cut the blood And then I made him tread the mud. Coy ma lin dow kill ko kill ko Coy ma lin dow kill ko me.

I fed my horse in a poplar trough (*3 times*)
And there he caught the whooping cough.
   Coy ma lin dow kill ko kill ko
   Coy ma lin dow kill ko me.

I fed my horse with a silver spoon
And then he kicked it over the moon.

Now my old horse is dead and gone,
But he left his jaw-bones ploughing the corn.

72 THE SWAPPING SONG
(*The Foolish Boy*)

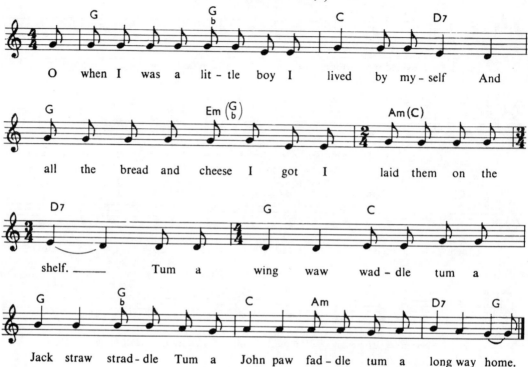

O when I was a lit-tle boy I lived by my-self And
all the bread and cheese I got I laid them on the
shelf. _____ Tum a wing waw wad-dle tum a
Jack straw strad-dle Tum a John paw fad-dle tum a long way home.

The rats and the mice they gave me such a life
I had to go to London to get me a wife.
    Tum a wing waw waddle tum a Jack straw
      straddle
    Tum a John paw faddle tum a long way home.

The roads were so long and the streets were so
    narrow,
I had to bring her home in an old wheelbarrow.

My foot it slipped and I got a fall
And down went the wheelbarrow, wife and all.

I swapped my wheelbarrow and got me a horse
And then I rode from cross to cross.

I swapped my horse and got me a mare
And then I rode from fair to fair.

I swapped my mare and got me a cow
And in that trade I just learned how.

I swapped my cow and got me a calf
And in that trade I just lost half.

I swapped my calf and got me a mule
And then I rode like a dog-gone fool.

I swapped my mule and got me a sheep
And then I rode myself to sleep.

I swapped my sheep and got me a hen
And see what a pretty thing I had then.

I swapped my hen and got me a mole
And the dog-gone thing went straight to its hole.

73 THE BIRD SONG

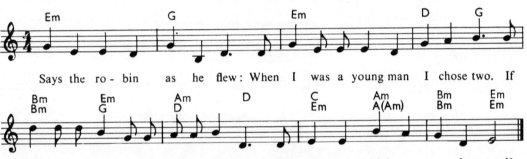

Says the ro - bin   as   he   flew: When   I   was a young man   I chose two. If

one did-n't love me the o-ther one would; And don't you think my   no-tion good?

Says the blackbird to the crow:
What makes white folk hate us so?
For ever since old Adam was born
It's been our trade to pull up corn.

Hoots! says the owl with her head so white:
A lonesome day and a lonesome night.
Thought I heard some pretty girl say
She'd court all night and sleep next day.

No, no, says the turtle dove;
That's no way for to gain his love.
If you want to gain his heart's delight
You must keep him awake both day and night.

74 TOMMY ROBIN
(Cock Robin)

Who killed lit - tle Tom- my Ro-bin, Who killed lit - tle Tom-my Ro-bin?

I, said the spar - row, with my lit - tle bow and

ar - row, It was I, O, it was I.

And it's who seen him die? (bis)
I, said the fly with my little streaky eye,
It was I, O, it was I.

And it's who made his shroud?
I, said the eagle, with my little sewing needle. Etc.

And it's who made his coffin?
I, said the snipe, with my little pocket-knife.

And it's who dug his grave?
I, said the crow, with my little spade and hoe.

And it's who carried him to it?
I, said the lark, with my little horse and cart.

And it's who laid him down?
I, said the crane, with my little drawing chain.

And it's who covered him up?
I, said the duck, with my little paddle foot.

And it's who preached his funeral?
I, said the dove, with my little morning love.

75 THE FROG AND THE MOUSE

The frog went a-court-ing and he did ride, H'm! h'm! The frog went a-court-ing and he did ride With his sword and his pis-tol by his side. H'm! _____

He rode up to Miss Mouse's door,
  H'm! h'm!
He rode up to Miss Mouse's door,
He off his horse and he boarded the floor.
  H'm!

I've come to ask will you marry me?
I live down yonder in the hollow tree.

O I have nothing to say to that.
You have to ask my Uncle Rat.

'Twas late in the night when the rat came home:
O who's been here since I've been gone?

A very nice gentleman here has been;
He asks me for to marry him.

Then Uncle Rat laughed and he chucked his fat
  sides
To think his niece was to be a bride.

Then Uncle Rat went galloping down to town
To buy his niece a wedding-gown.

O where will the wedding-supper be?
Away down yonder in the hollow tree.

O what will the wedding-supper be?
Two blue beans and a black-eyed pea.

The first come in was Miss Bess, old bug.
She carried a pitcher and a jug.

The next came in was a bumble-bee.
He tuned his fiddle on his knee.

The next come in was Mr Tick.
He ate so much that it made him sick.

Now we must send for Doctor Fly,
For I'll be dinged if Tick don't die.

Miss Mouse got scared and ran up the wall
And then she got an awful fall.

The cat came around and made a mighty splutter
And the rat got scared and ran up the gutter.

For specimen piano accompaniment see page 14

76 THE SQUIRREL

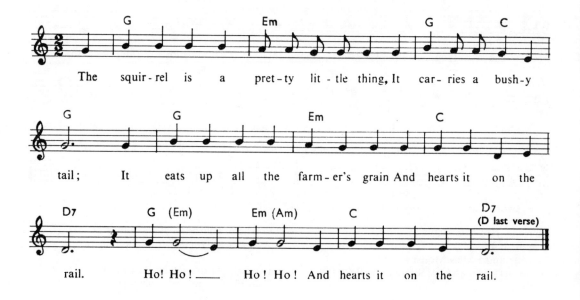

The squir-rel is a pret-ty lit-tle thing, It car-ries a bush-y tail; It eats up all the farm-er's grain And hearts it on the rail. Ho! Ho! ___ Ho! Ho! And hearts it on the rail.

The partridge is a pretty little bird,
It carries a speckled breast;
It steals away the farmer's grain
And carries it to its nest.
   Ho! Ho! Ho! Ho!
And carries it to its nest.

The racoon's tail is ringed around.
The opossum's tail is bare.
The rabbit's got no tail at all,
But a little bunch of hair.
   Ho! Ho! Ho! Ho!
But a little bunch of hair.

77 THE OLD WOMAN AND THE LITTLE PIG

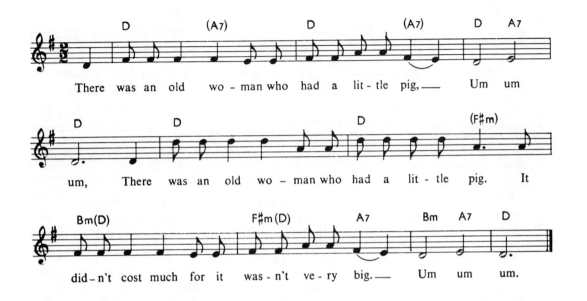

There was an old wo – man who had a lit - tle pig, — Um um
um, There was an old wo – man who had a lit - tle pig. It
did – n't cost much for it was - n't ve - ry big. — Um um um.

And this little pig it died in bed,
  Um um um,
And this little pig it died in bed.
It died because it couldn't get its bread.
  Um um um.

The old man died on account of grief.
O wasn't that a sad relief.

And the old woman grieved and she sobbed and
    she cried
And then she lay right down and died.

And there they lay upon the shelf.
If you want any more you must sing it yourself.

78 THE FARMYARD

* The passage between asterisks is sung twice in the third verse, three times in the fourth verse (the first time with variant), four times in the fifth verse and so on *ad lib.*

Had me a hen, *etc.*
The hen went ka, ka, ka, *etc.*

Had me a hog, *etc.*
The hog went kru-si, kru-si, kru-si, *etc.*

Had me a sheep, *etc.*
The sheep went baa, baa, baa, *etc.*

Had me a cow, *etc.*
The cow went moo, moo, moo, *etc.*

Had me a calf, *etc.*
The calf went ma, ma, ma, *etc.*

The song can be extended at will by adding the names and characteristic noises of other animals.

79   WHAT'S LITTLE BABIES MADE OF?

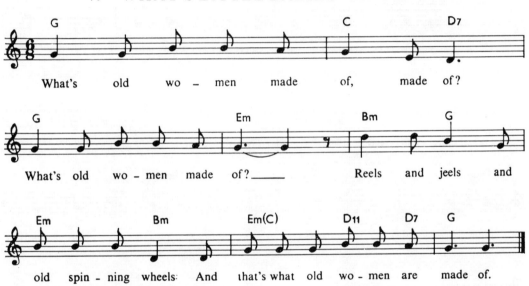

What's old wo – men made of, made of?

What's old wo – men made of?____ Reels and jeels and

old spin – ning wheels: And that's what old wo – men are made of.

What's old men made of? *Etc.*
Whisky and brandy and sugar and candy
And that's what old men are made of.

What's young women made of? *Etc.*
Rings and jings and all fine things
And that's what young women are made of.

What's little boys made of? *Etc.*
Piggins and pails and puppy dogs' tails
And that's what little boys are made of.

What's little babies made of? *Etc.*
Sugar and crumbs and all sweet things
And that's what little babies are made of.

For specimen piano accompaniment see page 12

80 THE BRIDLE AND SADDLE

NOTES ON THE SONGS

THE EIGHTY songs in this collection are published in *English Folk Songs from the Southern Appalachians*. Some of them have also been published with pianoforte accompaniment (see references below).

The tunes are printed as they were noted, without alteration. It has not been possible to treat all the texts in the same way for the singers did not always give us a complete set of words. When the text is incomplete or abstruse we have complemented it by lines or words from another version; sometimes we have wedded a tune to a text given by another singer; and in certain cases we have been obliged to make a compilation from various versions. With the exception of a few songs which have been supplemented by lines from versions noted in England, all the words are taken from Appalachian songs and in practically every case they are to be found in *English Folk Songs from the Southern Appalachians*. In the notes we have given particulars of any alterations we have made.

Nos. 1–29 are variants of what is generally known as the 'Child canon', i.e. Francis James Child's *The English and Scottish Popular Ballad*. This authoritative work deals almost exclusively with the texts. It has been supplemented by Bertrand Harris Bronson's *The Traditional Tunes of the Child Ballads with their Texts According to the Extant Records of Great Britain and America* (Princeton University Press, 1959–1966. In progress.). We have given the Child title in brackets where this differs from the title under which the ballad is more generally known, or the one which was given by the singer.

REFERENCES

The number in square brackets placed immediately after the song title refers to the number in *English Folk Songs from the Southern Appalachians* collected by Cecil J. Sharp, edited by Maud Karpeles (Oxford University Press, London, 1932, 1960). The capital letter following the number indicates the variant that has been selected.

FS of English Origin = *Folk-Songs of English Origin collected in the Appalachian Mountains* by Cecil J. Sharp with pianoforte accompaniment (Novello, London, 1919*, 1921. Published in one book, 1966).

Nursery Songs = *Seventeen Nursery Songs* collected and arranged with pianoforte accompaniment by Cecil J. Sharp (Novello, London, 1930).

Songs for Children = *Twelve Songs for Children from the Appalachian Mountains* collected by Cecil Sharp—pianoforte accompaniments by Imogen Holst (Oxford University Press, London, 1937).

* Volume I was published in America under the title of *American–English Folk Songs* (Schirmer, New York, 1918).

Child = *The English and Scottish Popular Ballad* edited by Francis James Child (1882–1898. Reprinted, Dover Press, New York, 1966).

Nine Folk Songs = *Nine English Folk Songs from the Southern Appalachian Mountains* collected by Cecil J. Sharp and Maud Karpeles with pianoforte accompaniments by Ralph Vaughan Williams (Oxford University Press, London, 1967).

1 *The Lovers' Tasks* (The Elfin Knight) [1A]. Child No. 2. Nine Folk Songs No. 3. Sung by Mrs Cis Jones at Manchester, Clay Co., Ky.

The third line in the last stanza has been taken from *Gammer Gurton's Garland*.

This ballad is one of the many examples of folk stories in which two people vie with one another in asking riddles or imposing impossible tasks on each other. The one who fails to find an answer or to make an equivalently difficult counter-demand usually has to submit to the will of the other.

2 *The False Knight upon the Road* [2A]. FS of of English Origin I No. 4. Child No. 3. Sung by Mrs T. G. Coates at Flag Pond, Tenn.

It is thought that this encounter between the boy and the knight is symbolic of the struggle between good and evil.

3 *The Seven Sleepers* (Earl Brand) [4G]. Child No. 7. Sung by Mr Clinton Fitzgerald at Royal Orchard, Afton, Va.

Only one stanza was noted from Mr. Fitzgerald and the present text has been compiled from other versions.

The expression 'better' which occurs in stanzas 5 and 8 is here used to emphasize the continuity of the action. According to Miss A. G. Gilchrist, the word is sometimes used in this sense in Lancashire.

4 *The Outlandish Knight* (Lady Isabel and the Elf Knight) [3F]. Child No. 4. Sung by Mrs Joe Vanhook at Berea College, Ky.

Stanza 1 has been taken from another version and in addition a few slight adjustments have been made in the text.

Child is of opinion that 'of all ballads this has perhaps obtained the widest circulation'. It is certainly one of the most popular ballads both in England and America. Cecil Sharp alone noted nearly sixty examples.

5 *The Two Crows* (The Three Ravens) [11B]. FS of English Origin II No. 5. Child No. 26. Sung by Mrs Ada Maddox at Buena Vista, Va.

6 *The Two Sisters* [5I]. Child No. 10. Sung by Miss Elsie Coombs at Hindman, Knott Co., Ky.

The text is mainly that given by Miss Louisa Chisholm at Woodbridge, Va. (FS of English Origin II No. 4).

In many versions of the ballad, a harp or other musical instrument is made out of the various parts of the dead girl's body and when it is played it sings the story of her murder.

7 *John Randolph* (Lord Randal) [7H]. Child No. 12. Nine Folk Songs No. 1. Sung by Mrs Ada Maddox at Buena Vista, Va.

She sang only a couple of stanzas and the present text is compiled from other versions.

8 *Edward* [8D]. FS of English Origin I No. 1. Child No. 13. Sung by Mr Trotter Gann at Sevierville, Tenn.

This ballad is generally known under the title of 'Edward'. The name does not occur in any of the versions we noted, but one singer told us that the man's name was Edward. We know from other versions that the conversation is between a mother and her son.

One of our singers expressed the opinion that the 'little piece of bush that soon would have made a tree' signified a young girl. An equally dramatic interpretation would be that the quarrel was about some insignificant matter which was out of all proportion to the ensuing tragedy.

9 *The Cruel Mother* [10C]. Child No. 20.
   Sung by Mr T. Jeff Stockton at Flag Pond, Tenn.
Only one stanza was sung by Mr Stockton and the present text is compiled from other versions.
   This is one of the most poignant of all ballads. There is probably no other ballad which attracts so many varied and beautiful tunes.

10 *Lord Bateman* (Young Beichan) [13G]. Child No. 53.
    Sung by Mrs Nanny Smith and Mrs Polly Patrick at Goose Creek, Clay Co., Ky.
A few verbal alterations have been made in the text.

11 *The Two Brothers* [12M]. FS of English Origin II No. 5. Child No. 49.
    Sung by Mrs Florence Fitzgerald at Afton, Va.
Only one stanza was noted from Mrs Fitzgerald and the present text has been compiled from other versions. For a fuller version, see 12F (also published in FS of English Origin I No. 2). In this version, the visit of the boy's true lover to his grave is described.
   In no other version is the cause of the killing made explicit. In most versions it might appear to be accidental, but from the following lines (version B) noted in Virginia it would seem to be jealousy:
   You're not the one that loves Susie
   And here I'll spill your blood.

12 *The Cherry Tree Carol* [15C]. Child No. 54.
    Sung by Mr William Wooton at Hindman, Knott Co., Ky.
The second line of the fifth stanza as given in our text occurs in most versions of the ballad and it gives point to the story. Mr Wooton sang it as 'All down unto them'.

The story is derived from the Apocryphal Gospel of S. Matthew. It is interesting that the Unborn Child predicts the date of His birth as January 5th. This, according to 'Old Style' reckoning was the date of Christmas Day between the years 1752 and 1799. Sometimes the reply given to Joseph's question is 'On old Christmas Day my birthday shall be'.

13 *Love Henry* (Young Hunting) [18M]. Child No. 68.
    Sung by Mrs Laurel Jones at Burnsville, N.C.
The text is as sung by Mrs Frances Carter at Beattyville, Ky. (see FS of English Origin I No. 3).

14 *The Maid Freed from the Gallows* [28A]. Child No. 95.
    Sung by Mr T. Jeff Stockton at Flag Pond, Tenn.
He sang the first stanza as follows:
   Hold up your hands and Joshua, she cries,
   And wait a little while and see.
   I think I hear my father dear
   Come lumbering here for to see.
'Joshua' or 'Joshuay' occurs in several other versions and may be a corruption of 'Judge' or 'Justice'.

15 *Lord Thomas and Fair Ellinor* [19M]. Child No. 73. Nine Folk Songs No. 2.
    Sung by Mrs Willie Roberts at Nellysford, Va.
Mrs Roberts sang only one stanza and the present text, with a few minor alterations, is taken from the singing of Miss Alice Parsons at Lincoln Memorial University, Harrogate, Tenn.

16 *Fair Margaret and Sweet William* [20L]. Child No. 74. Nine Folk Songs No. 4.
    Sung by Mrs Margaret Jack Dodd at Beechgrove, Va.
The text is an abridged version of the ballad as sung by Miss May Ray at Lincoln Memorial University, Harrogate, Tenn.

17 *The Three Little Babes* (The Wife of Usher's Well) [22B]. Child No. 79.
    Sung by Miss Linnie Landers at Carmen, N.C.

18 *Matthy Groves* (Little Musgrave and Lady
  Barnard) [23E]. Child No. 81.
    Sung by Mr T. Jeff Stockton at Flag Pond,
    Tenn.
  Only a couple of stanzas were noted from Mr
  Stockton and the present text has been
  compiled from other versions.

19 *Barbara Ellen* [24M]. Child No. 84. Nine
  Folk Songs No. 5.
    Sung by Mr Bin Henson at Barbourville,
    Ky.
  The text is taken from the singing of Miss
  Carrie Howard at Pineville, Ky.
    'Howdey' is the common form of greeting
  in the mountains. Other expressions occur-
  ring in the text, which are commonly used are
  'go about' (go near) and 'stair steps'.
    This is a favourite ballad on both sides of
  the Atlantic. Cecil Sharp noted 27 examples
  in England and 36 in the Southern Appalachian Mountains.

20 *Little Son Hugh* (Sir Hugh) [31F]. Child No.
  155.
    Sung by Mr Dol Small at Nellysford, Va.
  The text given here is as sung by Mr W. M.
  Maples at Sevierville, Tenn., except for slight
  adjustments in stanzas 2 and 8.
    This ballad, which has a long ancestry and
  is known in some form in many European
  countries, relates an incident which is sup-
  posed to have occurred in Lincoln during the
  thirteenth century in which a little boy named
  Hugh was said to have been tortured and
  crucified by the Jews. Such stories of ritual
  child murder have been told throughout the
  ages in many lands. They are, as Professor
  Child says, entirely without foundation and
  have been the pretext for many disgraceful
  acts of persecution against the Jews.

21 *The Death of Queen Jane* [32A]. Child No.
  170.
    Sung by Mrs Kate Thomas at St Helen's,
    Lee Co., Ky.
  Cecil Sharp told Mrs Thomas that the ballad
  she had just been singing related to Queen
  Jane Seymour who had died in giving birth to
  her son, Prince Edward, who afterwards

became King Edward VI. Whereupon she
triumphantly exclaimed: 'There now, I always
said that song must be true because it is so
beautiful.'

22 *Gypsy Davy* (The Gypsy Laddie) [33D].
  Child No. 200.
    Sung by Mrs Jane Gentry at Hot Springs,
    N.C.
  Mrs Gentry sang an incomplete version and
  the present text is collated with other versions.

23 *The Wife Wrapt in Wether's Skin* [39B].
  Child No. 277.
  Noted from Mrs Olive Dame Campbell who
  had learned the ballad from Miss Mary Large
  at Lee Co., Ky.

24 *Georgie* (Geordie) [34D]. Child No. 209.
    Sung by Mrs Laura Virginia Donald at
    Dewey, Va.
  The text has been collated with other versions.

25 *The House Carpenter* (The Daemon Lover)
  [35M]. Child No. 243. Nine Folk Songs
  No. 6.
    Sung by Mrs Virginia Bennett at Burns-
    ville, N.C.
  In some of the earlier printed versions the
  returned lover is a spirit, but this supernatural
  element does not appear in any of the sets we
  obtained in the Appalachian Mountains,
  although one may, perhaps detect some
  ghostly overtones.

26 *Our Goodman* [38E]. Child No. 274.
    Sung by Mrs Alice Sloan at Barbourville,
    Ky.
  Only one stanza was noted from Mrs Sloan.
  The present text was given by Mrs Tom Rice
  at Big Laurel, N.C.

27 *The Farmer's Curst Wife* [40B]. Child No. 278.
    Sung by Mr N. B. Chisholm at Wood-
    bridge, Va.

28 *The Weeping Willow Tree* (The Golden
  Vanity) [41A]. Child No. 286.
    Sung by Mrs Jane Gentry at Hot Springs,
    N.C.

29 *Fair Sally* (The Brown Girl) [44I]. Child No. 295.
Sung by Mrs Virginia Bennett at Burnsville, N.C.
Stanza 6 and the first two lines of stanza 9 have been taken from other versions.
It is open to question whether this ballad should be regarded as a version of The Brown Girl (Child No. 295). There are many common elements. The main difference, however, lies in a reversal of the sexes: in The Brown Girl it is the man and not the woman who falls in love, is taken sick and is spurned by the former lover.

30 *The Lady and the Dragoon* [51D].
Sung by Mr Clinton Fitzgerald at Royal Orchard, Afton, Va.
The text is taken from the singing of Mrs Sands at Allanstand, N.C.

31 *Locks and Bolts* [80A].
Sung by Mrs Rosie Hensley at Carmen, N.C.
The last stanza is taken from another version.

32 *Jack Went a-Sailing* [65A].
Sung by Mrs Jane Gentry at Hot Springs, N.C.
The fifth stanza is from another version.

33 *William Hall* [171C]. FS of English Origin II No. 7.
Sung by Mrs Margaret Dunagan at St Helen's, Lee Co., Ky.
Only one stanza was noted from Mrs Dunagan and the text has been compiled from other versions.

34 *William and Polly* or *Lisbon* [121B].
Sung by Mr Philander Fitzgerald at Nash, Va.
The text is a slightly shortened form of that sung by Mrs Jane Gentry at Hot Springs, N.C.
'Lisbon', the alternative title, is the one by which the song is often known. In other versions it is mentioned as the 'foreign land' to which William is bound.

35 *Sweet William* [106B].
Sung by Mrs Rosie Hensley at Carmen, N.C.
The text has been collated with other versions.

36 *The Cruel Ship's Carpenter* [49A].
Sung by Mrs Tom Rice at Big Laurel, N.C.

37 *The True Lover's Farewell* [114F].
Sung by Mrs Laura Virginia Donald at Dewey, Va.
Only one stanza was noted from Mrs Donald and the text has been compiled from other versions.
This is generally believed to be the song, or one of a similar type, from which Burns took many of the lines of his 'A Red, Red Rose'.

38 *The Cuckoo* [140I].
Sung by Mrs Florence Fitzgerald at Afton, Va.
The text has been collated with another version.

39 *Pretty Saro* [76A].
Sung by Mrs Mary Sands at Allanstand, N.C.
One stanza has been omitted.

40 *My Dearest Dear* [77]
Sung by Mrs Mary Sands at Allanstand, N.C.

41 *Black is the Colour* [85]. FS of English Origin II No. 12.
Sung by Mrs Lizzie Roberts at Hot Springs, N.C.

42 *The False Young Man* [94A]. FS of English Origin I No. 8.
Sung by Mr T. Jeff Stockton at Flag Pond, Tenn.

43 *The Dear Companion* [111]. FS of English Origin I No. 9.
Sung by Mrs Rosie Hensley at Carmen, N.C.

44 *The Irish Girl* [180A].
Sung by Mrs Frances Richards at St Peter's School, Callaway, Va.
The last two stanzas are taken from an English version noted by Cecil Sharp in Somerset.

45 *Come All You Fair and Tender Ladies* [118E].
Sung by Mrs Jane Gentry.
The text has been compiled from two other versions.

46 *Arise! Arise!* [57D]. FS of English Origin II No. 10.
Sung by Mr Alex S. Coffey at White Rock, Va.
The text is as sung by Mr Napoleon Fitzgerald at Beechgrove, Va., to an almost identical tune.

47 *The Nightingale* [145E]. FS of English Origin II No. 8.
Sung by Mrs Margaret Dunagan at St Helen's, Lee Co., Ky.
Only one stanza was noted from Mrs Dunagan and the text is as sung by Mr Chester Lewis at Lincoln Memorial University, Harrogate, Tenn.

48 *Green Bushes* [126].
Sung by Mrs Ada Maddox at Buena Vista, Va.
The text has been collated with a version noted by Cecil Sharp in Warwickshire.

49 *Good Morning My Pretty Little Miss* [107A].
Sung by Mrs Hester House at Hot Springs, N.C.
Some stanzas have been omitted and the last has been taken from another version.

50 *The Rebel Soldier* [157B]. FS of English Origin II No. 11.
Sung by Mrs Lawson Grey at Montvale, Va.
The first stanza is taken from another version and two stanzas have been omitted.

51 *The Rich Old Lady* [55A]. Nine Folk Songs No. 7.
Sung by Mrs Gosnell at Allanstand, N.C.

52 *Katie Morey* [115A].
Sung by Mr T. Jeff Stockton at Flag Pond, Tenn.

53 *I Must and I Will Get Married* [128].
Sung by Mrs Margaret Jack Dodd at Beechgrove, Va.

54 *Old Woman* (The Deaf Woman's Courtship) [178]. Nursery Songs, p. 16.
Sung by Mrs Emma Early at Clinchfield, N.C.

55 *Come My Little Roving Sailor* [205A].
Sung by Mrs Lucy Cannady at Endicott, Va.

56 *The Miller's Will* [161A].
Sung by Mr William Wooton at Hindman, Knott Co., Ky.

57 *Betty Anne* [88].
Sung by Mrs Ellie Johnson at Hot Springs, N.C.

58 *The Tree in the Wood* [206B]. Nine Folk Songs No. 8.
Sung by Mrs Frances Richards at St Peter's School, Callaway, Va.

59 *The Riddle Song* [144A]. FS of English Origin I No. 10.
Sung by Mrs Wilson at Pineville, Ky.

60 *When Adam was Created* [193].
Sung by Mr Jasper Robertson at Burnsville, N.C.
Mr Robertson was a Baptist preacher.

61 *Sinner Man* [208A].
Sung by Mrs Florence Samples at Beach Creek, Manchester, Clay Co., Ky.
This is a 'Holiness' song, i.e. a hymn sung at the meetings of a religious sect commonly known as the 'Holy Rollers'. The climax of the song is certainly a very telling one.

62 *The Crow-Fish Man* [199]. Nursery Songs, p. 5.
Sung by Mrs Wilson at Pineville, Ky.
This is a negro street-cry which Mrs Wilson had picked up. It was sung very slowly.

63 *Sally Anne* [240]. Songs for Children II No. 9.
Sung by Mrs Delie Hughes at Cane River, Burnsville, N.C.

64 *Cripple Creek* [241A]. Nursery Songs, p. 19.
Sung by Miss Lizzie Abner at Oneida School, Clay Co., Ky.

65 *Will You Wear Red?* [260].
Sung by Mrs Delie Hughes at Cane River, Burnsville, N.C.

66 *The Chickens They are Crowing* [269A].
Sung by Mr Ben Finlay at Goose Creek, Manchester, Clay Co., Ky.

67 *Going to Boston* [261].
Sung by Mr Hillard Smith at Hindman, Knott Co., Ky.

68 *Soldier Boy for Me* [272B]. Nursery Songs, p. 10.
Sung by Mr Jake Sowder at St Peter's School, Callaway, Va.

69 *Nottamun Town* [191A]. Nursery Songs, p. 2.
Sung by the Misses Una and Sabrina Ritchie at Hindman School, Knott Co., Ky. The singers are a sister and cousin respectively of Jean Ritchie, the folk-singer who has won fame in England as well as in America.

The song is published in *Folk Songs of the Southern Appalachians as sung by Jean Ritchie* (Oak Publications, New York, 1965). Here the two last words of stanza 2 are given as 'coal black'.

Nonsense songs, or songs of marvels or lies, as they are sometimes called, are much favoured among traditional singers. In many cases, they can be taken at their face value as mere fun, but 'Nottamun Town' cannot be thus dismissed. It conveys a sense of mystery, which although it cannot be explained is none the less real. Miss A. G. Gilchrist has contributed an interesting analysis of this type of song and its counterpart in folk-tales to the *Journal of the English Folk Dance & Song Society* (London, 1942).

70 *The Sally Buck* [159A].
Sung by Mr William Wooton at Hindman, Knott Co., Ky.

71 *I Whipped my Horse* [219].
Sung by Mrs Jane Gentry at Hot Springs, N.C.

72 *The Swapping Song* or *The Foolish Boy* [217A].

Noted from Mrs Olive Dame Campbell who had noted the song from a schoolgirl at Hindman, Knott Co., Ky.

73 *The Bird Song* [215A].
Sung by Mrs Jane Gentry at Hot Springs, N.C.

74 *Tommy Robin* (Cock Robin) [213B].
Sung by Mrs Ellen Webb at Burnsville, N.C.

75 *The Frog and the Mouse* [220B].
Sung by Mrs Jane Gentry at Hot Springs, N.C.
The text has been collated with another version.

76 *The Squirrel* [225B].
Sung by Mr Ebe Richards at St Peter's School, Callaway, Va.

77 *The Old Woman and the Little Pig* [235A].
Sung by Mrs Sophia Rice at Big Laurel, N.C.
The text has been collated with another version.

78 *The Farmyard* [218]. Songs for Children II No. 12.
Sung by Mrs Jane Gentry at Hot Springs, N.C.
The text has been collated with another version.

79 *What's Little Babies Made of?* [227A].
Sung by Mrs Mollie Broghton at Barbourville, Ky.

80 *The Bridle and Saddle* [224]. Songs for Children II No. 8.
Sung by Mrs Emily Snipes at Marion, N.C. Mrs Snipes told us that when her father sang to his children he always finished with this ditty. As soon as he started it they knew that they would not get another song out of him.

INDEX OF TITLES

INDEX OF FIRST LINES